THE SHADOW FALLS

Samantha had been in love with Greg since her early teens. When he realised that he felt the same, they set their wedding date. But suddenly, inexplicably, Greg postpones the wedding, becomes withdrawn, and disappears for days at a time. Slowly a grim, disquieting picture of Greg begins to emerge — after their hurried wedding ceremony, he is seen in the company of a mysterious woman. A stranger is lurking around, asking questions about Greg. And Samantha begins to fear for her new marriage — and for herself.

Books by Claire Lorrimer
Published by The House of Ulverscroft:

RELENTLESS STORM
A VOICE IN THE DARK
THE SECRET OF QUARRY HOUSE
THE SPINNING WHEEL

VARIATIONS:
COLLECTED SHORT STORIES

LAST YEAR'S NIGHTINGALE
THE SILVER LINK
FROST IN THE SUN
CONNIE'S DAUGHTER
HOUSE OF TOMORROW

ORTOLANS:
ELEANOR PART I
SOPHIA   PART II
EMMA   PART III

MAVREEN
TAMARISK
CHANTAL

CLAIRE LORRIMER

THE SHADOW FALLS

Complete and Unabridged

ULVERSCROFT
Leicester

First published in Great Britain in 1995 by
Severn House Publishers Limited
Surrey

First Large Print Edition
published 1998
by arrangement with
Severn House Publishers Limited
Surrey

British Library CIP Data

Lorrimer, Claire, *1921 –*
The shadow falls.—Large print ed.—
Ulverscroft large print series: romance
1. Romantic suspense novels
2. Large type books
I. Title
823.9'14 [F]

ISBN 0–7089–3941–4

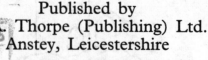
Published by
F. A. Thorpe (Publishing) Ltd.
Anstey, Leicestershire

Set by Words & Graphics Ltd.
Anstey, Leicestershire
Printed and bound in Great Britain by
T. J. International Ltd., Padstow, Cornwall

This book is printed on acid-free paper

Love is
a time of enchantment:
in it all days are fair and all fields
green. Youth is blest by it,
old age made benign:
the eyes of love see
roses blooming in December,
and sunshine through rain. Verily
is the time of true-love
a time of enchantment — and
Oh! how eager is woman
to be bewitched!

1

I cannot remember the first time I realized Greg had changed. In the beginning I really believed I was imagining it. Now I know very well that I was not. It is shattering to have to admit to myself that I am almost afraid of him.

I am trying very hard to be rational, to think things out coolly, unemotionally to be as fair as possible to Greg. Must I make the irrevocable decision to leave him? I'm finding it almost impossible, not just because there are so many imponderable, unexplained events but because I still love him.

I want to believe I am wrong; that he is neither cheating nor deceiving me; that our relationship is as important to him as it is to me; that he is not being cruel, neglectful, secretive.

I promised him on the eve of our marriage that I would trust him. Yet how can I? He has betrayed that trust too often.

There is no one in whom I can confide. Greg's Aunt Tibby will support Greg no matter what facts are put before her. Her blind adoration of him is equal only to her

1

jealous dislike of me! Nor can I tell my father. He would act without thinking of the consequences if he thought Greg had betrayed me and would behave as if he were still a naval commander court-martialling a young officer who had failed in the line of duty. Father would be even more prejudiced against Greg than Aunt Tibby was against me. As for my brother Jolly, he has been acting so strangely that I am afraid to question him. I am afraid of what he might say against Greg. Jolly — who was Greg's nearest and best friend all his life — Jolly has already advised me to leave him.

Reading that last paragraph in my diary, I realize that I am really a coward. In one sentence I want the truth; in the next I am afraid to hear it. I know why. I love Greg. I want to go on loving him. I cannot face the idea that for most of my life I may have loved a man who does not even merit my respect.

For that reason I am alone in my bedroom writing down my thoughts and feelings in the pages of an old school notebook. I hope this will clarify my mind.

In my infancy I used to toddle after my elder brother begging to be allowed to follow him and his friend Greg out into the garden or down to the beach to play. In those days

I think my adoration of both boys was equal. I remember I told my father that one day I was going to grow up and marry them both! I also intended to marry Father, whom I loved devotedly. I thought him very handsome. He had a certain presence and authority in his bearing, though he is on the short side and slight. His eyes, so used to peering out at a wide expanse of water, have lost much of their bright colour. But his thin face is still handsome. He was wonderful to us. He could be stern, though, barking out orders to us children as if we were sailors under his command. His anger was always justly deserved and we respected it.

By the time I was ten I was beginning to notice differences between the two boys. Jolly, like me, resembled our Italian mother. We were both dark-eyed, dark-haired, with the same creamy complexions that turned a deep, dark tan in the summer sunshine. We were, and still are, musical, a little over emotional. We are quick-tempered, but fast to get over our angers. We are extremists in our loves and hates, adoring our father and each other and Greg, and with equal passion hating a governess we once had. We are also moderately intelligent. Jolly graduated from Dartmouth with flying colours and I did equally well in school.

But if we were both bright, Greg was exceptionally so. It wasn't obvious when he was young. Fair-haired, fair-skinned, with brilliant, laughing blue eyes, he had a lazy, casual manner that hid the sharpness of his mind and his judgement. It was invariably Jolly who had the idea for some childish escapade but Greg who modified or improved or planned the great adventure. We were often in trouble. Jolly was looked on as the ringleader, but in fact Greg was by far the stronger character of the two boys. As I grew up, I realized that his failure to shine at school was entirely voluntary. He did not wish to outshine Jolly and be moved into a different section or put a class ahead. Jolly had to work hard for results. Greg's school reports reiterated over and over again: *He could do better. Doesn't try!* In one way it was absolutely true. He could, if he tried, always leap ahead of Jolly.

By the time I was turning from child into young woman, I think I was already in love with Greg. A word of praise from him and I was happy for the rest of the day. Because my sole aim in life was to be permitted to share the boys' lives, I naturally became a tomboy. The only time Father ever smacked me was the day I cycled into the village and had my long dark hair cropped short so I could look like a boy. I tried to do everything the boys did: row a boat, fish for lobster and mackerel, repair the outboard engine, clean the boat, climb trees, scale the rock cliffs. I did most things almost as well as they could. I think they put up with me because I was always useful. To both of them I was a kid brother rather than sister, and I was happy to have it that way.

Until my teens. Then, when I knew I was in love with Greg, I wanted him to realize that I was a girl. It seemed he never would. If I wore a skirt instead of my usual tattered jeans, he'd merely scowl and say, "How on earth do you think you can climb for gulls' eggs in that ridiculous outfit? Better go home and change."

That would send me rushing home in abject misery. I'd fling myself on my bed and weep tears of mortification. But because I was young and healthy and not yet quite out of my childhood, I'd end up changing into my oldest things and running back down to the beach.

Those years were ideally happy for all three of us. Our house, Tristan's Folly, was a long stone building erected by my grandfather, William Jolland, as a bridal gift for my grandmother. Despite all local advice, he insisted on building the place

5

out on the headland on the cliffside, close to the rocks against which the Atlantic seas beat mercilessly day and night. He paid a small fortune to construct the long, low-turreted house, despite the coastguard's warning that when winter came, it might suffer severe damage, especially when the sou'westers blew.

Grandpa stubbornly insisted that Tristan's Folly was indestructible. But when that first winter did come, the storms were a fury of destruction; terraces were washed away, timbers snapped, shutters torn from their hinges, carpets and furniture soaked by the giant waves and hopelessly discoloured by salt water.

It was the same every year. My grandfather would survey the debris and ignore it, sitting unperturbed in his library waiting for the first cuckoo of spring. Then he would rebuild his house. He spent a small fortune repairing, restoring, repainting his home. He was an immensely rich man, and the constant outpouring of money seemed not to concern him. When the sun once more shone on the mussel-covered rocks, and the terraces were vivid with great tubs of flowering plants, he would lie on his chaise longue and watch the passing ships through his old telescope and talk to my grandmother. There was soothing music from the waves gently lapping the foot of the rocks below them. The villagers became used to the eccentric aristocrat and many of them relied on the annual repair work as a regular part of their livelihood.

All this was history my father recounted to us children many times. When young, we took the winter's onslaught on our home as much for granted as we took the spring influx of workmen. Jolly and I loved the Folly as much as my father did, and I suppose one day, when Father dies and Jolly is married, he and his children will live there. We are fortunate in that the family fortunes are in trust and secure. Barring some unforeseen disaster, there will always be enough money to keep Tristan's Folly going.

Greg's home is almost in total contrast to mine. Tristan's Bay, a beautiful curved stretch of pale golden sand, is not very far from Bedruthen Steps on the north coast of Cornwall. Trevellyan Hall, built in the early part of Victoria's reign, lies in the most sheltered part of the bay. It is barely half a mile from the Folly. It is a square white house with a garden full of green trees and shrubs and flowers and bird song. I suppose it could be called the manor house of the district. It has none of the weird atmosphere or charm of Tristan's Folly but is solid and comfortable, furnished with shabby Victorian furniture and old chintzes. The Trevellyans lost their money when Greg's uncle, a businessman, gambled the family fortune away in an Australian gold-mining venture after the First World War.

Greg's parents died about the same time as my mother, soon after I was born. Greg's Aunt Tabitha, came to live at the Hall and look after the little boy. I sometimes used to be frightened of Aunt Tibby. She could be so cold and sarcastic. Her face frightened me, too: it's hatchet-shaped, and she has narrow penetrating eyes and a wart on her chin with hairs on it. But she had, and still has, a slim, graceful figure, and she can smile suddenly when she is in a good mood. In those days she was kind as well as cruel. In those days she didn't like me. She preferred my brother. Greg she adored.

When she first went to live at the Hall, it was an act of great personal sacrifice. As a young girl she had been engaged to my father, and the wedding day was only a few weeks off when he met my mother. He fell madly in love with her and virtually eloped with her, leaving poor Aunt Tibby jilted and broken-hearted. She never forgave him. Unable to stand local gossip and sympathy, she went to live with a cousin in Scotland

and no doubt would have remained there but for the death of Greg's father. Duty brought her back to live once more in Tristan's Bay. She never married.

But I could never truly dislike her; she had such total, unselfish love for and devotion to Greg. For that I tolerated her, and Greg adored her. That she hated me he shrugged off with a laugh. "You're your father's daughter, Samantha. How *could* she like you?" he'd say reasonably enough. I felt sorry for her, especially when Greg finally fell in love with me and told Aunt Tibby he was going to marry me.

But that is leaping too far ahead of my story. I think it began when I was on convalescent leave from the hospital in Newquay where I was training to be a nurse. I had had an attack of glandular fever during the summer and was living at home with Father. This was when Greg finally noticed me as a woman. I think it was the happiest time of my life. I was virtually in heaven.

It was the night of the annual entertainment of the Cavern Concert — an event of great interest to locals and tourists alike. It took place in the great cave beneath the west headland of Tristan's Bay when the cavern would be dry for the best part of an hour before the tide came rushing in. A mini piano was dropped by ropes through a hole in the roof onto a stage formed by a natural platform of rock at one end of the cave. A hundred people could attend, and stand in the cave, each holding a lighted candle.

Whenever I was at home for this particular event, I was invited to sing. I could accompany myself on my guitar, and though I was untrained, I suppose from my Italian mother I had inherited an ear for music. That evening I was not in any way excited at the prospect of the concert because Greg and Jolly were away. They were both at a naval establishment in South Cornwall. No event had much meaning for me if Greg were not present. But to please my father, who had begun lately to take pride in my appearance and frequently told me how like my mother I was growing, I took trouble with my clothes, wearing a deep crimson skirt and white full-sleeved blouse that showed off my tan, acquired after a lazy summer in the sunshine. I pinned my long dark hair on top of my head.

Before I left the house, I stared at the oil painting of my mother that hung in the hall. How like the woman I'd never known I was in feature and colouring. Perhaps, I thought, she could have told me how to make Greg fall in love with me as passionately and instantly as my father had fallen in love with her!

I wasn't the only one to be thinking of Greg. As Father and I climbed slowly down our rocky path to the sands — he suffered sometimes from arthritis and could not move with his former agility — he took my arm and said:

"You look very lovely, my dear. My little duckling has really blossomed into a swan! I wonder what young Greg will think of the transformation!"

"I don't suppose he'll notice, far less approve!" I said. I spoke tartly to hide my embarrassment at the compliment and shyness because he had inferred I had changed my appearance to attract Greg.

Father smiled.

"If he doesn't see it he'll be as blind as a bat and far from the hot-blooded young fellow I think him," he replied.

Suddenly I felt miserable.

"Such speculation hardly matters very much, Father, since Greg won't be at the concert!" I muttered. He did not reply, but pointed to a lone seagull flying low across the gentle, white-rimmed waves that lapped the outgoing tide.

"The most beautiful spot in the world!" he said sighing. "I could never live anywhere else. Even after your mother died, I never considered moving away from Tristan's Bay. You, Jolly, Greg and I, we're all children of the sea. And you, my dear, are like this place — beautiful! I'm proud of my Samantha."

I felt a sudden rush of love for him. And I thought he was so right about Tristan's Bay. Our roots were indeed firmly planted here. Mine had been an idyllic childhood, my nineteen years the happiest a child could know. If only . . .

The crowd was filing into the cavern. We went in as twilight fell. Their many candles flickered and glowed, illuminating the interior of the cave in a mysterious and beautiful way. The wet walls glittered. The acoustics in the cave were magical, slivering the music. As Father and I entered, a girl student who taught the local children the piano, was playing Beethoven's Moonlight Sonata. I made my way to the platform to stand with the other performers to take my turn, and thought of the brilliant yellow harvest moon that would later flood a path over the sea and across the lonely sand dunes. Soon I would have to return to work at the hospital, and my chances of seeing Greg on one of his rare leaves would be considerably lessened. Tears suddenly filled my eyes. I brushed them away and greeted my fellow musicians as cheerfully as I could.

Farmer Penreddy, who had a deep bass voice, sang one of his ballads. Miss Tremence, the organist at the little chapel, played her favorite Chopin prelude. The next on the rota was the primary school master conducting a trio of students. The person to perform before I did was old Dai, the Welshman who had made his life here on the Cornish coast. He took his place on the platform and sang a song he had set to music. His voice, a wonderful mixture of Welsh and Cornish dialect, lent an added excitement to words I already knew so well:

And all night long the stone
Felt how the wind was blown
And all night long the rock
Stood the sea's shock;
I looked out and wondered why
Why at such length
Such force should fight such strength.

I felt the words and the deep, rich cadence enter my heart and touch me with a great melancholy. Then someone whispered that it was my turn, and I picked up my guitar and stepped onto the platform, into the glow of a hundred candles.

I had chosen a Brazilian song about the mountains. It had a gay yet haunting melody. My heart lifted, and I was carried away as I looked at the many tanned weather-beaten faces before me, most of them familiar and dear. Some of the people in the audience hummed the chorus with me. I smiled as I sang and played the last chorus, my voice sounding as impressive as a great soprano's as it echoed from the rocky roof.

Then I saw Greg. He was with Jolly near the entrance to the cave, tall, slim, beautiful, in his uniform. He was watching me, a half smile curving that wide laughing mouth I loved so much.

The blood flared in my cheeks. My heart jolted and my voice faltered just for a second. Then, with wild exhilaration, I concluded my song. My long dark hair tumbled down from its pins and fell across my face. I sang and played for Greg.

Minutes later he was beside me, pressing my arm against him, lacing his fingers with mine. Neither of us spoke. We stood together through the rest of the performance until someone shouted:

"All out!"

The tide had turned. The audience began to run in single file out onto the shadowed sand. Strong arms had already begun to hoist the piano up through the roof. The candles guttered and went out. The concert had ended for another year.

Jolly took my other arm. Father was talking to the landlord of the Saracen's Head so we began our walk across the sands without him. Still no one had spoken. Then Greg said to Jolly:

"Beat it, old boy. Two's company, three's a crowd!"

The amazement on Jolly's face can only have equalled my own. We had always, always done everything as a threesome.

"Jolly, I would like to talk to Sammy *alone!*" Greg said calmly and slowly, a glint of a smile in his eyes.

Jolly's face broke into a grin.

"Okay, okay!" he said. "I know when I'm not wanted!"

With a laugh he turned and strolled back toward Father. Greg and I began to walk. Suddenly he took a firmer hold of my arm and said:

"Six bells!"

It was our kid's code word for danger, and the formula was always to run for the nearest cover. I had been trained early by the boys never to ask questions when the warning was called but to run as fast as I could after them and ask why later. So now

I instinctively grabbed my skirt, kicked off my shoes, and, barefoot, chased after Greg toward the sand dunes.

He ran a good deal faster than I could. Greg was now six foot three, and his long legs could always give him the advantage. By the time I reached the sand dunes I had lost sight of him. The next thing I knew, I was tumbling head first into the sand. Greg had brought me down with a tackle, and I fell so suddenly and heavily I was winded and stunned.

His voice roused me from my stupor.

"Darling, I'm so sorry. *I'm so sorry!* Sammy, are you all right? Darling, Sammy. Answer me!"

Even had I the wind to reply, the totally unaccustomed endearment would have silenced me. I felt his arms lift me. The next moment my head was cradled against his shoulder, and he was gently brushing the sand from my eyes and mouth. His fingers were indescribably tender.

I lay very still, my heart hammering furiously.

"God, you're in a mess!" I heard his soft chuckle. Then he put his hand beneath my chin, lifted my face up to his, and kissed me.

I will never forget that moment. No matter

what happens in the future, I cling to the memory of that split second of time. Just before Greg's lips touched mine in the first kiss he had ever given me, I saw his blue eyes, laughing, filled with love. I *know* he loved me then. I have to keep thinking of it so that I can believe these last months are a nightmare and that other moment the reality.

When Greg finally stopped kissing me, he explained that he and Jolly had suddenly been given leave and had decided to hurry home in Jolly's car to be in time for the concert. It was to have been a surprise for Father and me. But it had turned out to be a surprise for Greg: he'd seen a girl singing on the platform in the cave and had fallen in love with her. Only then had he realized that I was the girl.

"I suppose I've always been in love with you!" he said, kissing me again. "Only I didn't know it. I just didn't see you had grown up. You're a beautiful, desirable, attractive, fascinating, wonderful, wonderful girl. Sammy, for pity's sake say something. Tell me you care just a bit about me. Why don't you answer me?"

It was my turn to laugh. I explained that with a mouthful of sand, half winded, and suffocated by his kisses, I had hardly been able to speak. But if he would stop kissing me long enough to let me do so, I'd tell him I loved him, too, had loved him for years and years and that I'd never love anyone else as long as I lived.

I couldn't say any more even if I'd wished to because Greg began kissing me again and suddenly his kisses became more violent, and I felt an answering passion so violent that it was a kind of pain. I had not realized love, physical love, could be so furious and so intense. I had no will to resist Greg as he began to explore my body. I wanted his hands on me. I wanted to touch him. I wanted to belong to him in every possible way.

It was Greg who broke off before the moment became totally out of control. He was trembling as violently as I was, and his voice was hoarse as he said:

"We must get married, Samantha. As soon as possible. I love you. I shall always love you. I have always loved you. Oh, *darling*!"

Then we were kissing again, but gently, tenderly, our hearts on our lips.

"I suppose it sounds silly, but I'd like to die right now," I whispered to him. "I'm so happy I know I could never again be more so."

Greg hugged me closer.

"That's the Latin in you speaking. We aren't going to die, darling. We're going to live. Perfect, long years together. I'll make you a thousand times happier than you are now." Greg kissed me again and pulled me to my feet. "We're going straight back to Tristan's Folly. I want to ask your father's permission to marry you," he said. "You will marry me, won't you, Sammy?"

As if I could have said no.

We fixed our wedding to take place in the village church a month later. But that, once again, is getting ahead of my story.

2

Father opened a bottle of vintage brandy and put his arm around Greg's shoulders.

"Was beginning to think you'd never get around to it, my boy!" he said happily. "Knew it would end up like this. Just didn't think it would take so long."

Greg laughed sheepishly.

"I can't understand it myself," he said, holding my hand. "I suppose Sammy was too close for me to see her as anyone but Jolly's kid sister." He turned to Jolly and added: "This will make us brothers-in-law, John Jolland. How about that!"

I looked from one to the other with stupefied content. How lucky I was to have a brother like Jolly! He was less handsome than Greg, being short and sturdy, but so like his nickname — amusing, his wide mouth made for laughter. I maintained that I had a better nose. It was short but moderately well shaped.

My brother was grinning.

"Remember when we cut our fingers to mix blood to make us blood brothers, Greg? Sammy was furious because we wouldn't let her be a 'brother' too!"

There were so many shared memories! Swimming, surfing, at which we were all expert, climbing, exploring the caves, looking for gulls' eggs Father so enjoyed eating. Then there were the children's parties when one of the three of us had a birthday. Those had been special days for me because it was traditional for the birthday boy or girl to have any rational desire granted. It meant on one day of the year I could monopolize Greg's time and attention fully.

Father reminded me that I would be twenty in a month's time, and by mutual consent it was agreed Greg and I would get married on that day. Neither of us felt any need for an engagement. We already knew each other well enough! There remained only Aunt Tibby to give her approval.

"Won't be easy!" Father said laconically. "I'm afraid Tibby won't break her vow never to speak to me again, not even at your wedding!"

Greg disagreed.

"I know my aunt is still very bitter, sir," he said. "But no matter how she feels, she won't let anything spoil my happiness. She has always put me first, as you know. And despite her feelings about you, she has never once barred the door to Jolly and Sam."

21

"She didn't bar the door exactly," I said, "but she never really made us welcome, Greg. Me in particular."

"Probably because you look too much like your mother!" Father said bluntly. "You *are* like her, Samantha — more and more so as the years go by."

"Was Aunt Tibby ever beautiful?" Jolly asked my father curiously. "One can't imagine it now."

"She *was* a very good-looking young woman," Father informed us. "She still has her neat figure and trim ankles, not that I suppose you notice such things. But she's let herself go. Should have had that wart taken out but wouldn't let a surgeon touch it. Now it's a real disfigurement. Her eyes were never big and beautiful like your mother's, Sam, but they were bright and mischievous. She could look a treat at a party, and she danced well — wonderful waltzer. Terrible how people can change. Tib had more than one admirer. Unfortunately she had eyes only for me. Great pity." Father looked very sad. "It keeps me awake at night sometimes, remembering that I virtually ruined her life. It's the one regret I have about the way I lived my life. Not that I could have shaped events differently. I truly believed I loved Tibby until I met Caterina. If only Tibby could have forgiven me and married someone else!"

"I think she enjoys her bitterness in a twisted kind of way," Greg said. "It's a kind of compensation for love — hating you, I mean. It must have taken a great deal of courage for her to return to the scene of her humiliation when my mother died."

"For which I've always admired her," Father agreed. "She's been a wonderful 'mother' to you, Greg. I just hope this engagement won't upset her too much. Maybe it will finally bring us together again. We are both lonely old people, and it would be very gratifying to end up friends."

I began to feel the first nigglings of doubt. Aunt Tibby's ceaseless jibes about my father whenever an opportunity arose were so much a part of everyday life that none of us took any notice. When winter came she would listen almost with glee to the wind rising and announce smugly: "Tristan's Folly will be under water again before long. Your father's as mad as his father, Samantha. Be drowned, the lot of you one of these days, in your beds most likely." Or if I mentioned that Father's arthritis was worse, her dry comment would be: "Drinks too much. Always did, silly old man!"

Greg, Jolly, and I would catch each other's eye and grin. Tibby's jibes meant nothing. But my proposed marriage to Greg was different. The mere idea of a wedding between the two families might open old wounds, and for the first time in my life I understood how deep they were. If Greg ran off with another girl before our wedding, I'd want to die. There certainly wouldn't seem any point in living if Greg were forever lost to me.

I looked at him as he held out his glass for Father to refill. He looked totally unconcerned, his face radiant and glowing. I wondered what would happen if Aunt Tibby really set her heart against our marrying. Greg adored her. He had every reason to do so. I appreciated how much she had done for him and could even love her because she loved him. We had that much in common. I made a silent resolve to be as gentle, understanding, and tactful with her in the future as I could be.

"Shall we go to the Hall and tell Aunt Tibby the good news?" Greg asked me suddenly.

My courage failed. I couldn't bear anything to spoil what must surely be the happiest moments of my life. If there was to be any trouble, let it come tomorrow.

Greg took my refusal in good part without

asking for reasons. He had several of his own.

"Aunt Tib doesn't know I'm on leave," he said. "So if I don't put in an appearance at home, she won't miss me. With your permission, sir, I'd like to stay here at the Folly so I can see as much of Sammy as possible before Jolly and I have to go back on Friday."

Father shrugged his shoulders.

"I understand how you feel, boy, but you're forgetting that half the local population, if not all of it, saw you at the concert. Someone will mention it to your aunt, and then the cat *will* be amongst the pigeons. Best go home tonight, Greg, break the news to her as gently as you can, and come back here in the morning. If Tibby takes it well, Samantha can go home with you to lunch."

"Now I know why you were such a good commander, Father!" Jolly said laughing. "Diplomatic and intelligent!"

We dined very late in the beautiful room overlooking the sea that Father loved so much. The bay window had been fashioned like those of old sailing ships, and when one stood gazing out of the casements, there was no sight of land. The oak dining table shone with polish lovingly applied daily by old Elsie, the Cornish woman who had worked for us all her life. The table was nearly black with age and stood proud and solid on the soft, sea-green carpet that had discoloured with the years of salt spray and cleaning into a misty gray-green that no man-made dye could have emulated.

My mother had collected many fine paintings. These hung on the walls in their gilded frames. The most beautiful of all was a Renoir that hung over the big stone fireplace.

All through the meal and afterward when we drank coffee in the drawing room, I was conscious of Greg's eyes, never for long away from me. I knew he found me attractive, and the knowledge made me feel more so. I, in turn, could not keep my eyes from his beloved face. Friday, when he would leave me, was like a stone in my heart, and I felt I had to imprint on my mind every line and contour of his face. Not that I did not know them already! But now it was with a heightened awareness, a physical consciousness that had not really been part of loving him before. I had always harboured romantic day dreams. Perhaps they sprang from physical desire, but I had not been conscious of it. Now Greg's kisses had made me fully aware of my body, and it yearned for his. Even as it does now, when I am ashamed because I still want him in spite of everything.

But that evening I wanted him to want me, and I know that he did, for later, when I walked part of the way back to Trevellyan Hall with him, he led me once more into the deserted sand dunes and told me feverishly that he could never wait a whole month for me.

This time I was the one who kept control. I knew Greg would regret it if we gave way to the urgency of our need for each other. He and Jolly had often discussed girls as if I were indeed not a girl myself. They were both romantic and spoke scornfully of the 'easy' ones, the village girls who called after them in the street or who followed them out of the pub. They might banter with them, even flirt with them, but love them — never! I'd never been jealous of these girls whom I knew only by sight and name: Annie, the publican's daughter, Mattie, the boat builder's youngest girl who waited on table at the Saracen's Head, Hetty, who sold souvenirs to summer visitors. The girls were all young and pretty, and Greg and Jolly were the most eligible young men in the village. I might have been jealous if I had not heard them discuss these poor girls so disparagingly.

Eventually I walked all the way to Trevellyan Hall with Greg. The great harvest moon had risen and was flooding the sand and grass and gardens with a soft silver sheen. It lit up the mass of Virginia creeper that covered the walls of the house. I was looking at Greg's face as we walked through the garden. He reminded me of a beautiful bronze Greek god. I wondered how I would ever be able to say good night and leave him. He, too, had the same thought about me, for he suddenly laughed and said:

"*You* can't walk *me* home, my darling. *I* should be seeing *you* home. Turn around and I'll walk you back to the Folly."

He insisted on coming home with me. But this time, by unspoken consent, we did not stop by the dunes. We held hands, and it was, inexplicably, enough. Greg quoted me one of his favourite poems. He wrote it out for me later, and I have kept a copy. It was written by Sir Samuel Ferguson and had the strange Celtic name of *Cean Dubh Deelish*

Put your head, darling, darling, darling,
Your darling black head my heart above
Oh, mouth of honey with the thyme for
* fragrance*
Who, with heart in breast, could deny
* you love?*

"I always loved that poem," Greg said. "Perhaps I knew when I first read it that one day I would marry a dark-haired girl."

"But you never thought of marrying *me*?" I asked.

Greg smiled at me in the moonlight.

"Of course I did, silly! But I put the thought out of my mind pretty quickly. I didn't want a wife who could scratch and bite and kick like an urchin every time she lost her temper, or swear like a Cornish fisherman, or climb the walnut tree quicker than I could. Or," he added, laughing as I gave his hair a vicious tug, "pull my hair whenever I teased her."

"Greg, be serious. Did you *ever* think of marrying me? Honestly?"

"Yes, darling. But only because I saw you as a lifelong companion and friend. I always loved you. But tonight I fell in love with you. So you see, I have everything I want all in one parcel. Sammy, enough of the way I feel about you. I want to know when *you* first knew you loved *me*, really loved me, I mean!"

We must have lingered an hour or longer on that ten-minute walk home, exchanging lovers' nonsense. We both laughed at the thought of Jolly's face if he could hear us. As children we had all scorned sentimentality,

29

yet here were Greg and I behaving like love-sick kids. Not that either of us felt ashamed of it. The moon-in-June had nothing on our moon-in-September!

I fell into bed and was at once asleep, exhausted by a surfeit of happiness and emotion. The last drop of contentment filled my overflowing cup when I found a note on my pillow from my brother saying: 'Terribly glad for you both and for myself.' Dear Jolly. Now we three need never be separated for long.

The morning brought the first breath of chill, not just in the autumn air that seemed suddenly keener, colder. It showed on Greg's face when he arrived in time for lunch. I knew at once that he had had a difficult morning with Aunt Tibby.

He took me out onto the terrace and told me that his aunt's reaction had been totally unexpected. She had not been angry; nor did she even voice an objection to our marriage. She had sat down in one of the old rocking chairs in the kitchen and cried.

"I didn't seem able to stop her," Greg said. "It was painful. It was as if all the years of grieving for your father suddenly burst the dam of her pride, and she was overcome."

I felt quite overwhelmed and waited to hear more. Aunt Tibby eventually calmed down, he said, and told him that she had always suspected this would happen, that she had nothing personal against me, and that if I loved Greg as much as she believed I did, she would not try to stand in our way. At the same time, she could not face the thought of sharing her home with me, and Trevellyan Hall could not have two mistresses. Greg soon discovered the rest of the truth. She feared that I would want Father to visit, and this would be unendurable for her. She, therefore, felt she must leave the Hall and Greg and return to Scotland to live with her cousin again.

Greg finished urgently:

"You must dissuade her, Sammy. She has made her life here in Tristan's Bay, and Trevellyan Hall is her home. I know she would be tearing herself in pieces if she went away."

"I'll try!" I promised. But in my heart I couldn't believe Aunt Tibby's decision to go would be altered by any persuasion from me. She was right in supposing that I would want my father to come and see us in what would be my home when I married Greg. If she could not swallow her pride and put the past behind her . . .

"I'll try," I promised again, inwardly resolving to put the facts fairly and squarely before Aunt Tibby. She and Father *must* end their quarrel. Father had nothing but pity for her but had naturally respected her wish not to speak to him. He was used to her cutting him if they saw each other in church or in the village, though it never failed to upset him when this happened.

After lunch I took Father into the library and prevailed upon him to write a note to Aunt Tibby that I could take with me when I went to the Hall later on. Father didn't think it would help much, but to please me he wrote it all the same.

Dear Tibby,

I know you can never forgive me for hurting you as I did, but for the children's sake, could you not see your way to letting bygones be bygones? Greg is devoted to you and would miss you very much indeed if you were to leave the Hall. Samantha has no wish for you to go, either. Personally I would be very happy if we could be friends once more, not just for their sakes but for my own.

Sincerely,
William Jolland

I had no way of knowing what Aunt Tibby thought of that letter. She read it and threw it on the kitchen fire. The expression on her thin, lined face remained inscrutable.

Greg went out to saw logs, which, we had agreed, would be the best way of leaving Aunt Tibby and me alone. I plucked up my courage and told Aunt Tibby I really did wish she would change her mind and stay on at Trevellyan Hall.

"Not just for Greg's sake, but for mine, too," I said. "I would very much like to continue with my nursing training. I cannot run the Hall and pursue my career. Greg and I both need you here. Please stay."

I must have struck the right note, or else Father's letter had meant more than she betrayed to us. Her expression remained inscrutable, but she sounded quite friendly, if somewhat surprised as she asked:

"You intend to go on nursing after you are married?" I nodded.

"Unless Greg is posted somewhere where we can have married quarters, we are likely to be separated for months at a time. I'd be very bored doing nothing but looking after this house. Then there is the matter of wasting the training I have had so far. And there is a shortage of nurses. I think I ought to go back to the hospital for a while, anyway. Until I could have a child, perhaps."

33

Suddenly Aunt Tibby's expression changed. I thought I saw a softer look in her eyes, and her mouth trembled slightly. She struggled to remain her old hard self.

"Much too young to have children yet!" she barked. "Too young to get married if you ask me. But that's your business. Oh, well, I might stay on here for a while. I'm not promising. We'll see."

I went out to Greg, jubilant. It looked as if we'd won. If we were careful and didn't force Father's company on her too obviously, maybe she'd accept him too. They would have to meet at the wedding. It would happen then in the natural course of events.

The remainder of Greg's leave was idyllic for both of us. I even felt secure enough in this new-found love to put on my jeans again for one afternoon! Greg, Jolly, and I spent a crazy day fooling around on the beach like children. We made a driftwood fire and toasted marshmallows. We jumped the rising waves and ignored the threatening grey storm clouds. When they burst open drenching us, we stripped off all but the minimum of clothing and ran up and down the shore with our hair and faces streaming with rain and salt spray, laughing, shouting, and tripping over one another.

But all the time Greg and I were conscious of each other, our excitement heightened by these newly awakened senses. We outran Jolly into the shelter of one of the caves and kissed violently and passionately before Jolly caught up. He found us standing innocently a yard apart. Greg did not dare touch me again for fear of igniting the flame that flared between us.

When the rain became less torrential, we climbed the rock path home and had hot baths. In the library we toasted crumpets in front of the fireplace. The storm outside gathered momentum, and the room darkened, illuminated only by the firelight. Father said:

"Looks as if winter has come!"

Greg and I didn't care. I don't think Jolly did, either. He seemed as happy as we were.

We played Monopoly. Father cheated, as he always did if he thought he was going bankrupt, and the game disintegrated into shouts of "Unfair, unfair." Father got out the sherry, and we drank toasts: to the Queen, to the navy, to ourselves, to the Folly, becoming more childish and stupid until we were toasting the sherry decanter! Father told us to behave, and we dissolved into giggles. Greg and I held hands; then

Greg asked me to play my guitar and sing for him.

I sang three love songs. I sang with my heart and with my soul and with all the love I had for him. I stopped only because I saw tears in Father's eyes. I suddenly knew he was desperately lonely for my mother. I felt then that my love for Greg would be as enduring as Father's had been for my mother. Since she had died, he had been entirely faithful to her memory, and although he very seldom showed emotion, I understood now how empty the years must have been for him, especially when Jolly and I were away at boarding school.

We left Jolly with Father for company and went back to dine with Aunt Tibby at the Hall. She had prepared a wonderful roast duck meal for us.

After dinner we sat in the comfortable, shabby drawing room, and Aunt Tibby softened toward me sufficiently to show me her album of photographs. They were nearly all of Greg, a plump, handsome baby with golden curls and the same laughing blue eyes. I did not remember the toddler, but the little sturdy boy was instantly familiar to me. Jolly and I appeared in an occasional snapshot, perched on the garden wall with Greg between us, up the old apple tree, wearing shorts and T-shirts, or riding the white pony who was now nearly thirty years old and living out his remaining years in the orchard.

I was amused to see myself, distinguishable from the boys only by my size. I looked quite as grubby and unkempt as they. Greg kept calling me 'urchin,' though I could see that he was touched by those snapshots, which betrayed my urgent desire to be one of them.

"I suppose Jolly and I made life pretty tough for you!" he said as Aunt Tibby closed the album. "We never made allowances for the fact that you were a girl."

"She was happy enough," Aunt Tibby said shrewdly. "The only time I ever saw Samantha cry was when you two ran off and left her behind. So long as you let her tag along she was happy."

I could remember the desolation of being deserted and unwanted, but I had forgotten until now how gentle and kind Aunt Tibby was to me on those occasions. Usually so forbidding, she would take me into the kitchen with her, and gave me some dough to make pastry men, or allowed me to shell peas or stir the precious plum jam. I could see now that in her severe, dictatorial way she had felt sympathy for the tearful little girl.

Impulsively I reached out a hand and covered her thin one; covered the one ring she always wore, an old fashioned and rather lovely opal. I wondered if Father had given it to her.

"You were good to me in those days, Aunt Tibby. I want to thank you."

"Nonsense!" she said sharply, although her eyes smiled. "I thought you were a thoroughly undisciplined, headstrong little girl with few manners and a wretched temper. A most objectionable child!"

Greg laughed. I found myself smiling. Somehow I knew Aunt Tibby would never have confessed such feelings for me if she had not secretly liked me.

"You really didn't approve of me, did you?" I teased.

The words were unfortunate. An uncomfortable silence held the three of us as simultaneously we found ourselves remembering that my mother, whom I so closely resembled, had stolen the love of her life. No wonder Aunt Tibby resented me.

"It's no good harping on what's past!" Aunt Tibby said eventually, surprising us again. "It's the future that matters now, and you'll have to start thinking, Samantha, about the way you wish to refurbish this house. There's never been money enough to keep it up as it should be kept, so I dare say you'll want to make quite a few changes."

Instantly I denied it. This was Greg's home. Shabby and threadbare though it was, it was the way we'd both always known it. My first reaction was that I wouldn't want to change a thing. Aunt Tibby had taste, and there were some lovely pieces that had belonged to the family for years. A thick Persian carpet — very valuable — covered the whole floor. A rosewood cabinet was filled with precious china. There were several beautiful paintings. As I looked around me, I found myself admiring but not feeling as at home as I did in my own little tower bedroom, my mother's simply decorated drawing room, or my father's 'den,' packed with photographs, trophies, pipes, chests of cigars, and his collection of old guns. Trevellyan Hall was Greg's home, not mine. But I wouldn't change it for that reason alone.

Aunt Tibby virtually pulled the rug of sentimentality out from under me.

"Never heard such nonsense. Those satin-brocade curtains are so thin they won't stand another cleaning. They'll have to be replaced in any case. It's up to you and Greg to choose something you both like. And the rooms — all the rooms — are far too cluttered. I've been thinking, Greg. I've a little bit of money saved for a rainy day, and if you and Samantha agree, I might use it to convert the old stable block into a small flat. Then I could move some of the knick-knacks I'm fondest of out of the house and at the same time have a bit of privacy. Kill two birds with one stone."

Greg and I fell in with her idea. Two women in one household seldom worked in practice, and it would give Greg and me a chance to be on our own. I did wonder, though, if this could be Aunt Tibby's way of ensuring that she would not meet or have to make her peace with my father.

"If that's what you want, then that's what we'll do," said Greg. "I'll see Pentyre before I go back to the base tomorrow. He can give us an estimate for the work. I dare say we'd get a grant of some sort for adding a bathroom and kitchen. If you are sure it's what you want, Aunt Tibby?"

"I'll give it some more thought, but I'm fairly sure," she replied.

So everything was arranged. Next morning we saw Pentyre, the builder, and — even more exciting for me — saw the vicar and asked him to read our banns. Our wedding day was fixed for the twenty-fifth of October — my birthday and exactly a month away.

There was one more thing Greg wanted to do in Tristan's Bay. I seemed to be seeing the village with new eyes as I walked through it that morning with my hand tightly held in Greg's. It was a straggling old-fashioned-looking cluster of houses at the foot of a hill. It boasted a church, one post office, a general store, a butcher's shop and, of course, the Saracen's Head Pub. We did have one modern touch — the garage and some petrol pumps. The little primary school was situated farther up the hill. In the center of the village was the square in which the weekly market was held. It was here Greg wished to go.

It was market day and, refusing to tell me what he wanted, Greg disappeared into the jostling crowds. People were buying or selling fruit, vegetables, cream, flowers, eggs, poultry — anything and everything.

When Greg finally reappeared, he was carrying something in his arms. He was looking cheerful and triumphant.

"For you, darling!" he said, handing me a small bundle of black and white fur.

"It's supposed to be a springer spaniel puppy," he added, watching my face. "I thought he could belong to both of us."

I cuddled the puppy with delight. I'd

41

wanted a dog for years, ever since Frisky, our old Labrador, had died. No one had had the heart to replace Frisky until now.

"I expect your father will take care of him when you go back to the hospital," Greg said as we began to walk home through the village. He had thought it all out during the night. "If not, I know Aunt Tibby will look after him. What shall we call him, Sammy?"

I looked into the melting softness of brown eyes, at the shining wet nose, and I cuddled the little animal closer as I fell swiftly in love with Greg's present to me.

"You choose a name," I said.

"Nothing fancy!" said Greg thoughtfully. "Let's give the little brute a good sound masculine name like William!"

So William it was. We took him home to show Father; he looked at him doubtfully for a moment and then started to give us instructions on how to rear him. I knew then that William had been accepted. Jolly, of course, was at once crazy about him.

All too soon it was lunchtime. Immediately afterward the boys had to leave for their naval base. I walked back to the Hall with Greg and waited with Aunt Tibby while he went upstairs to change into his uniform. The minutes seemed to be rushing by now as the moment came for Greg to leave me. I felt my heart sinking. So much had happened in this brief leave that I had not had time to consider how I would feel when Greg went out of my life again.

He came downstairs looking suddenly older and to me incredibly handsome in his blue uniform. He had a last surprise for me.

"It was my mother's," he said, reaching into his pocket and bringing out a very beautiful antique diamond and emerald ring. "For our engagement. I hope it fits, darling."

It might have been made for me. Greg slipped it onto my finger and kissed me.

Aunt Tibby cleared her throat and said sharply, "I hope you aren't superstitious about emeralds, Samantha. Some folk think a green stone unlucky."

Greg and I laughed. At least, I started to laugh, but whether I had had too great an emotional upheaval these last two days, or whether I was just overtired or upset at the thought of Greg's departure, I don't know, but my laughter turned to tears. Even with Greg's arms holding me tightly, I was horribly aware of a strange chill pervading my body, seeping into my mind.

"Darling, *don't*, please!" Greg begged me, distressed. "If you don't like the ring, I won't mind a bit. We'll choose another one, Sammy . . . "

I hastened to reassure him that it wasn't the ring that was upsetting me, merely the thought of his going away.

"That's nonsense!" Greg told me as my sobs subsided. "I'll phone you every evening, darling, and Jolly and I will almost certainly get a weekend off before my wedding leave." He looked at my tearful face anxiously. "The trouble with you is that you really aren't one hundred per cent fit yet. I can't remember when I last saw you cry, darling." He grinned as he added: "That's girl's stuff, and you're one of *us*, remember?" His reminder of our childhood made me smile.

Aunt Tibby, who had tactfully made herself scarce, reappeared now with a tray of tea things. We just had time to drink a cup of strong tea before Jolly's car horn sounded in the drive.

Having my brother there made the actual moment of parting easier. The two boys joked and ragged each other the way they used to do when the end of the holidays came and they were going back to school. I was reminded of the same sinking of my heart I used to experience each time I waved them off down the drive.

I'm being silly! I told myself as Jolly drove Greg away from me. *I should be the happiest girl in the world.* Yet I was not. Try as I might, I could not rid myself of a strange sense of foreboding.

3

My apprehension soon disappeared during the busy days that followed. I prepared for my wedding. There were invitation cards to be bought and sent off, some to the many nurses I trained with, some to school friends I still saw occasionally or kept in touch with by letter. Greg had sent me a long list of brother officers he wanted me to invite to the wedding. Over the telephone we speculated on how many romances we might start between nurses and naval lieutenants.

Then there was my trousseau to buy. I went to Newquay for the day and chose my going-away outfit and lingerie, and I needed a new bikini and thin summer dresses to wear on our honeymoon in Madeira. It was likely to be warm there even in October.

Father had given me a more than generous cheque for all I wanted. I found slacks, and shirts to wear with them. At another shop I was lucky to find a full-skirted cotton dress, navy blue with white polka dots and a scarlet belt. It was very feminine. I found a sheath dress in the palest yellow with a halter neck that would leave my arms and shoulders bare to show off the tan I hoped to acquire abroad.

My wedding dress was to be made by the local seamstress, one of Aunt Tibby's few friends, who did fine work. I thought about it carefully beforehand and decided to risk reviving painful memories and ask Aunt Tibby to help me choose the material and style. I need not have worried because she entered, enthusiastically for her, into the choice and supervised the first fitting.

We decided on a chiffony kind of material, white, in a very simple style with a small collar, long tight sleeves, and a wide ruching at the hem and cuffs. With it I would wear the pearl necklace and pearl earrings that had belonged to my mother, and her Limerick lace wedding veil with a circlet of artificial orange blossom. At the first fitting, as I stared at the reflection in the mirror, I thought it couldn't be me. But it *was* me, and I was happy because I was sure Greg would like the transformation of his untidy tomboy into this new feminine me.

I was kept busy by William, who had to be house-trained, a fairly exhausting job especially as the weather was bad. It rained so hard nearly every day that I had to steel myself to put the little silky-haired puppy into the garden. He was very intelligent and quick to grasp what was required of him, but nonetheless there were plenty of accidents.

Greg telephoned me every evening as he had promised, until one evening when his six o'clock call did not come through. I was not unduly worried until eight o'clock the following evening. It looked as if Greg had once again forgotten to telephone me.

Father noted my restlessness.

"He's probably on a course or even at sea," he reminded me. "A naval officer's wife can't be too demanding or possessive, my dear, as you'll soon find out."

I took this reproof to heart. Greg would certainly not like a wife who kept hourly tabs on his movements. I would like to have spoken to Jolly just to reassure myself that Greg was not ill, but I forced myself to keep far away from the telephone.

However, on the third night of silence from Greg I put through a call to the officers' wardroom. The steward informed me that Mr. Trevellyan was away but that Jolly was available. My brother came to the phone and told me that Greg had gone to London.

"He didn't say why — in fact, he told me to mind my own business," Jolly said laughing. "Probably got a blonde mistress stashed away, and he's gone to say goodbye to her!"

48

"Jolly!"

I suppose the tone of my voice made him realize I had lost my sense of humour.

"Really, Sam, there's nothing to get worked up about," he said. "I'm sure Greg will ring tomorrow. And we may be coming home next Wednesday. Tell Father and Aunt Tibby, will you?"

My anxiety turned to joy. Greg would be back with me in a few days' time. How stupid of me to worry the way I had, and how stupid of my brother to talk that way about Greg. I'd have known if Greg had a girl . . . Not that Jolly had meant it; it was his way of teasing me.

But *would* I have known? The question niggled at the edge of my mind for the rest of the evening. I was unable to concentrate on my game of chess with Father, and he beat me easily. I realized that while Greg had been living at the Hall, I'd known all his friends and activities, but he'd been away at college for years and for the past year at H.M.S. Trenoun, while I had been away doing my training. Greg could have had several different love affairs and I would not have known about them. He was tall, strong, intelligent, with a wonderful sense of fun and an alert, inquiring mind. He had immense charm. I could not believe any female in her right mind would fail to find him attractive.

For the first time in my life I knew what it was to be miserably jealous. Jealousy was a trait I had always despised in other people and vowed I would never permit in myself. I had seen one unpleasant version of it in an extreme case at the hospital. The wife of one of the surgeons had haunted the building, shamelessly keeping tabs on her husband, who she thought was chasing one or other of the pretty nurses. It was not only acutely embarrassing for him but for everyone on the staff who could not ignore her pathetic inquiries as she tried to check up on her husband's whereabouts. We none of us knew how he stood it and still remained gentle and loving with her. The strain on him was enormous, and we all felt it was only a matter of time before his work would be affected.

I was horrified to imagine myself turning into this kind of wife to Greg and there and then resolved never to be jealous or suspicious again.

I meant that resolve. Yet here I am, eaten away by suspicion that I cannot explain or justify. And this despite my promise to Greg that he could always count on my unquestioning trust. How easy it had been to give that promise, how impossible to live up to it. I still want to trust Greg, but I cannot. Even Jolly has lost faith . . .

I think back to that evening when I spoke to Jolly on the phone. That was when I felt the first twinges of uneasiness. Or did my doubts really begin on the day Greg told me he wanted to postpone our wedding? When he came home with Jolly that Wednesday, he told me he could no longer get the two weeks' leave he had been promised, so our honeymoon could not now take place.

"We'll just have to postpone the wedding," he said, as if it were of no great consequence to either of us.

"But I don't see why, Greg. We can still get married even if we have to postpone our honeymoon until you do get leave."

I expected Greg to hug me and console me. Instead, he walked away from me and stood staring out at the angry waves crashing on the rocks below the dining room window.

"I think it would be best to postpone the wedding altogether," he said quietly. "If we can't have our honeymoon, then I'd rather wait to get married until we can."

I was glad his back was toward me so that he could not see my face. I was bitterly hurt and disappointed.

"But surely the powers that be would give

51

you a day off for our wedding . . . " I began. Greg's voice was cold, without even a trace of emotion as he broke in:

"Yes, but I'd *prefer* to postpone it, Sammy. I think it would be best."

I didn't understand. On his previous leave he had seemed as impatient as I for our marriage.

"The invitations have gone out!" I protested.

He turned and came across the room to me.

"I know it will be an awful nuisance for you, darling, but we'll just have to notify everyone of the change in plans."

His quiet resolution left me no room for more argument. There was a determination and a finality in his decision that I could neither understand nor fight against. Pride, of which I had plenty, prevented me from trying to talk him round.

The ensuing two days of his leave held the strangest mixture of happiness and misery I had ever undergone. At one moment Greg would seem remote, unapproachable, almost as if he were regretting he had asked me to marry him, almost as if he wasn't really in love with me. Then he would take me in his arms and kiss me with such a violent and desperate passion that we were both swept out of control.

"I love you, I love you. I want you so much!" he said over and over again.

I was terribly tempted to give way to the surge of passion. My body certainly had no will to resist him. Set at the back of my mind I knew that I must not betray my basic principles. There was nothing except Greg's inexplicable reluctance to prevent us getting married in two weeks' time. If he really needed me so desperately, he would overcome whatever strange scruples he had about marrying me despite the postponed honeymoon.

I left it to Greg to tell Father the news. He sounded awkward and embarrassed as he did so.

"I know Samantha doesn't entirely agree with me at the moment," Greg said, "but I feel it will really be better for her if we postpone our wedding for a little while."

If Father was surprised he didn't show it, although he knew me well enough to see the confusion and disappointment on my face. Jolly was less reticent.

"Can't see why you can't get married and go on a honeymoon later on," he innocently repeated my argument. "Lots of people prefer to do that, anyway. Why on earth postpone the wedding at this stage?"

Greg's mouth set into a stubborn line.

"I don't want half measures for Sammy," he said. "I want everything to be perfect."

I tried to cling to that thought — that Greg had reached his decision, however mistakenly, believing it was best for me. But after he had gone back to Trenoun, I realized he had never once consulted me, asked me what *I* wanted.

I did not go to see Aunt Tibby. I was beginning to identify myself with her as the jilted bride. I could not fight off the idea that Greg was trying to back out of the engagement, that he was beginning to regret his impulsiveness.

I took a long, solitary walk on the rain-swept, deserted sands, William tumbling along on his little legs beside me. Next day I went for a final fitting of my wedding dress. It was quite beautiful but now merely made me want to burst into tears.

Greg wrote to me.

Darling Sammy,
I love you. I shall always love you. I think of you constantly and miss you dreadfully. No matter what happens you must believe that. I think trust is very important between lovers, and I want you to trust me absolutely even if you can't always understand why I do or say things

that don't make sense to you.

Please write to me, dearest, and tell me you love me as much as ever. I can't help it, but I am feeling very depressed.

Your devoted, Greg.

It was the first letter I had ever had from him. And I was torn in two by it. Half of me melted into sheer unquestioning response, while the nasty little worm in my mind said: *It's your fault, Greg, not mine, if you are depressed and your leave was spoilt.*

But the desire to make him suffer a little as I delayed replying to him was finally undermined by my true unselfish love for him. I couldn't bear to think of him as unhappy, my laughing, loving Greg. So I wrote, telling him that I loved him as much as ever, that a honeymoon was not important to me. All I wanted was to belong to him and please, please would he let me set another date for our wedding very soon.

I watched every post for his reply, but I had to wait two whole days before his letter came. When it did, it was a bitter disappointment. He avoided any mention of a wedding date, saying only how much he loved me and missed me, but that it was unlikely he or Jolly would get leave before Christmas.

Father found me in the library weeping my heart out. Bit by bit he extracted the facts from me. He looked worried but spoke as if he were not.

"You've got to remember that you've been in love with Greg for a long while," he told me gently. "But Greg has only just discovered his feelings for you. It's natural for him to want a little longer to be quite sure how he feels. Marriage is a big step and an important one. It shouldn't be taken on impulse."

His words, however well intentioned, only succeeded in unnerving me further. I now knew that Father, too, believed Greg was having second thoughts about marrying me.

"It's even possible Greg has Aunt Tibby's misfortunes at the back of his mind," Father went on. "I was quite sure I wanted to marry poor Tibby until I met your mother. Greg knows the story well enough. He may feel he owes it to you as well as to himself to wait a while longer. Be patient, my dear. I'm sure he loves you. It isn't in your own interest to force him to marry you before he is ready for it."

I was sure now only that Greg wanted me, wanted to make love to me. Although innocent of any sex experience, I had been long enough with medical students, doctors,

56

and student nurses to know quite a bit about the difficulties of distinguishing physical passion from love. Like all youngsters, we girls had theorized on the subject for hours on end. We had all agreed that sex was a vital ingredient of a happy marriage but that no marriage could be guaranteed to succeed if this were the only ingredient. Was this, I wondered now, what Greg feared?

As I waited through the long weeks to Christmas, bought presents and wrapped them, decorated the house, tied ornaments on the Christmas tree, I alternated between hope and despair. Greg occasionally telephoned, but he wrote once or twice a week. He continued to reiterate his love for me but never once mentioned a new date for our wedding. I felt suspended in mid-air. I think the only thing I really took an interest in was my puppy, William, now my adoring and adored shadow. He was full of fun, and romping with him I could forget my tortured mind and enjoy a carefree hour or two.

Pentyre had gone a long way toward converting the stable block into a flat for Aunt Tibby. I went to see her twice a week and found her surprisingly enthusiastic as she showed me the latest improvements. It was as if she were suddenly beginning at this late stage of her life to permit herself to feel pleasure. Her grim, stern expression had softened, and she had put on weight almost as quickly as I was losing it. The doctor had insisted that my sick leave be prolonged another two months. He felt hospital life would be far too strenuous for me in view of my slow recuperation.

I packed my trousseau away in Father's old sea chest. I couldn't bear to look at the polka dot dress, the sexy nightgowns, my crimson dressing gown — all the pretty clothes I had never yet worn. As I folded them in tissue paper, I felt close to weeping.

By mutual agreement, Father and I never spoke of the marriage. But I continued to wear my engagement ring.

Quite suddenly it was the week before Christmas. Greg and Jolly were due home on the twenty-third of December, but Jolly came in time for dinner on the evening of the twenty-second. Greg, he told us, was following by train the next day.

I wore black slacks and a shirt. Jolly, as usual, brushed his hair and cleaned his nails but did little else to show that he was at a dinner table. Only Father 'dressed.' He wore his threadbare velvet smoking jacket, which he refused to part with despite its age. He looked very distinguished, his white beard and hair gleaming in the candlelight.

Through dinner both Father and I noticed that Jolly seemed unusually quiet. Father asked him if he was feeling well.

Jolly looked strangely embarrassed.

"I'm okay!" he said. "A bit over-tired, I expect. All those exams have worn me out!"

Jolly had always had to slog to pass exams, so Father accepted the excuse, but I was close enough to my brother to know there was something more than tiredness affecting him.

We had our first chance to talk alone when Father went up to bed. We sat on either side of the blazing log fire, and I broke the silence with a question Jolly must have been waiting for.

"How is Greg?"

The look Jolly gave me could only have been described as solicitous.

"I don't know, Sam. To tell you the truth, I'm worried about him. It's one of the reasons I shot off home without him. I felt I ought to warn you."

"Warn me? About what?"

Jolly's face screwed up in confusion.

"That's just it. I can't tell you. I only know that he's changed. You know how things have always been between Greg and me. We've never in our lives done anything, one without the other. I suppose we've been as close as any pair of identical twins. I wouldn't think of going down to the pub without him or nipping up to London for a show if he couldn't come too. He was the same with me. But these last weeks he has been avoiding me, making excuses not to join in what I was doing, not inviting me when he had something in mind."

Jolly leaned forward and looked directly at me.

"I thought I was imagining it at first, but I now know I am not. Greg has changed. He's quieter, more reticent, almost secretive. I have the feeling he's hiding something from me, but I can't imagine what. I'm thoroughly disturbed."

I tried to stop the trembling of my hands. I was afraid Jolly might hear the furious beating of my heart. After a moment I had sufficient control of myself to smile at him and say lightly:

"Perhaps he's fallen in love with one of those glamorous Wren officers you told me about and thinks you'll disapprove. After all, he is engaged to your poor little sister!"

I expected Jolly to smile back at me and laugh off the ridiculousness of my suggestion. But his face remained grave.

"I don't think there's a Wren on the scene.

But . . . well, a fellow officer started kidding Greg in the wardroom the other night about a redheaded woman he'd seen Greg chatting with in the Red Lion. The chap was only ragging, and I thought Greg would laugh and tell us all who the redhead was. But he went quite white and clammed up completely. I was shaken, I can tell you; and a bit worried, too. Coming on top of his strange behaviour and the postponed wedding, I began to worry a bit about your part in all this, Sammy. I don't want you to get hurt. Much as I love old Greg, I'd kill him with my bare hands if he hurt you."

"There's probably a perfectly simple explanation for all of it," I said, to reassure Jolly. I, myself, felt beyond reassurance. "Let's wait till Greg comes home tomorrow. We'll know soon enough if he wants to break off the engagement."

Jolly looked at me, as well he might, with surprise.

"You're taking this incredibly calmly. Do you mean it wouldn't shake you all that much if Greg did want out? I thought you *really loved* him, Sammy."

Somehow I kept outwardly calm, cool, under control. Inside, my heart was screaming in protest.

"Of course I do. I've always loved him,

and I dare say I always will. But that's no guarantee he feels the same way about me, and if he doesn't, then naturally I wouldn't want to marry him."

Jolly let out his breath, a whistling sound that frightened me more than anything he had so far said or done. It was as if he were saying to me; "*Thank goodness this isn't going to throw you because I'm pretty sure Greg does want out!*"

I don't think I slept at all that night. I both longed for and dreaded Greg's arrival.

When finally he appeared at tea time, my heart melted as from my bedroom window I watched him leap the steps two at a time and push open the heavy iron-studded oak door. He was wearing slacks and a polo-necked fisherman's jersey, so I knew he had first gone home to see Aunt Tibby and change out of his uniform. There was no rain today, but a fierce gale was beating against the walls of the house and had ruffled Greg's fair hair into an untidy mop. His face looked unusually grim.

I waited a few minutes, gathering together the remnants of my courage before I went downstairs to face what I now felt to be inevitable — Greg's change of heart.

I was, therefore, totally unprepared when without a trace of self-consciousness, ignoring both Father and Jolly, he hurried across the drawing room and swept me into his arms.

"Darling, *darling!*"

They were the only words he spoke, but I could feel his heart thudding against mine, and the way he was holding me, it was obvious he never wanted to let me go.

Father and Jolly must have decided to make themselves scarce because when Greg finally released me, they had disappeared. Greg sank into Father's enormous leather armchair and pulled me down onto his lap.

"Oh, Sammy, I've missed you so terribly!" he said in a gruff voice. "Tell me you still love me. Tell me nothing has changed. Say it! Say it, darling!"

There was so much urgency in his voice that although I failed to understand the need for it, I at once kissed him and told him I loved him as much if not more than the last time I'd seen him. In all the confusion of my feelings this much I knew for sure.

"I'll always love you, Greg. I always have and I always will."

Greg's face broke into a radiant smile. But it was soon replaced by an expression of stern concentration.

"I've got to talk to you, darling," he said, his voice low and serious. "It's very important. I've been thinking a great deal about us, about the way we love each other. As you know, I thought it might be best to wait a while, but I can't bring myself to accept an indefinite delay. I want you to be my wife. I want it more than anything in the world."

I closed my eyes, finding the transition from fear to joy almost unbearably acute.

"I don't understand, Greg," I said after a minute or two. His arms were still around me. To think more clearly I moved slightly away from him. "If we both feel the same way about getting married, what is there to stop us? Why should you have thought it better to wait? You haven't explained this to me."

It seemed a simple enough question, yet I could read in Greg's face the difficulty he had in replying. My former fear returned. I took a deep breath.

"Greg, if there is someone else, or has been someone else, perhaps someone you thought you were in love with and aren't sure . . . "

I got no further, for his face broke into an amused grin as he said easily:

"That's a crazy idea, Sammy. I've never loved any girl before you. You know that. Whatever gave you the idea?"

I prevaricated, not wishing to betray Jolly's confidence.

"It was the only reason I could think of why you might wish to postpone our wedding."

Greg no longer smiled.

I waited for him to give some explanation, but it did not come. The silence between us lengthened. I could see the struggle in Greg's face and feel his indecision.

I finally broke the silence.

"Whatever it is, surely you can tell me? Trust me?"

"I *can* trust you, can't I, Sam? I know that. But do you trust me? Can you trust me absolutely?"

I felt the importance he attached to my answer, so I thought very carefully before I replied:

"If you tell me it would be right for me to do so, why, yes — I'd trust you totally and absolutely."

Greg had been holding his breath. As I spoke, I could hear the tension rushing out of him in a long sigh.

"Then that's the way it's got to be, darling. There may be times when my words or actions don't make sense to you, and I may not be able to explain things to you. There may even be times when you think I don't love you. I can't explain now. But I do love you. I want to marry you. I want to get a special licence and marry you before Christmas. I have no right to ask you to do this, but . . . "

"No right?" I picked up the words, frowning. "But surely if you love me, and if I love you, right doesn't come in to it."

"It's a question of whether it is fair to you, darling. I can't explain. It's the beginning of this question of trust. You've got to accept what I say and trust me blindly, I suppose. That isn't easy. It won't be easy. It could even be very, very difficult. If I had the slightest doubt about the depth of your love for me, I know our marriage would be impossible."

Questions, dozens of them, were burning on my lips. I was completely confused and it seemed to me that Greg was almost as confused as I was. The only single irrefutable fact that I could cling to was that we loved each other, that we both wanted to get married. If his demand for blind trust was the only thing standing between us, then he could have it.

How simply and calmly I gave my promise. I meant it and believed I could fulfill it. But I never knew how hopelessly difficult it would be. I never foresaw the terrible strain it would put on our love, on my happiness, on my peace of mind. It is only because I did make that promise that afternoon in the quiet room with the wind raging outside and the log fire flickering that I am still Greg's wife. Otherwise I would have left him months ago. I could not go on trusting him when again and again he betrayed that trust, used my promise to evade explanations for conduct that no ordinary wife would accept.

Yet I still love him and am ashamed of the weakness of my heart.

4

We were married in Newquay registry office on Christmas Eve, Father and Jolly our only wedding guests.

It was a small bleak room, newly built and with a lot of new light wood and a strong smell of polish. There were several little pews for the witnesses and a large desk behind which the registrar officiated. He was a nice enough man, grey-haired, bespectacled, small, and rather fussy. As we approached his desk I was shivering with nerves. I held tightly to Greg's hand. He wore his uniform, and I, a small thinnish figure, stood trembling beside him in a blue dress and jacket with an imitation fur collar and a Russian-style fur cap on my head. There were red roses on the registrar's desk. They had been sent by Aunt Tibby. She had refused to be present. The excuse she gave was that she did not approve of registry office weddings, but I think the real reason was that she was unprepared for the thought of meeting Father. She told me, though, that she would come to my 'real' wedding, taking it for granted we would have our marriage blessed in church some time in the future.

I, too, wanted the church ceremony. This was more like a civil contract than a wedding. Remembering my beautiful white wedding dress, I comforted myself with the thought that I could wear it one day soon.

Now I am glad our wedding was so short and impersonal, without any feeling of reality. It seems to me that nothing about our marriage is real, anyway.

Yet on that cold Christmas Eve I was happy enough when Greg slipped the wide gold band onto my finger and we drove home in the back of Jolly's car, arms about each other, Greg's eyes filled with love and happiness. I was not thinking of the future then, only of the present and that I was by some miracle married at last to the man I had adored all my life, that tonight I would lie in his arms and become truly his.

Because Greg's and Jolly's leave was so short and because I did not want to leave Father and Jolly to cope with Christmas alone, Greg and I were not going away. Father had suggested we occupy the guest wing, a little suite of three rooms: bedroom, bathroom and sitting room. I had spent the entire previous day keeping fires alight, airing the rooms, rearranging the furniture, to make a warm and private place for Greg and me.

I don't think Greg would have minded very much where we were provided we were together but, typically female, I wanted the setting to be beautiful.

There was a force nine gale blowing as we rounded the headland and drove to the comparative shelter of Tristan's Bay. Father gave a professional glance at the sky and warned Jolly to be careful as we climbed the hill to the Folly. The waves were enormous, bubbling with white foam on their crests, spilling it higher and higher up the rocks as they sought to drench our lonely house.

Father laughed.

"They're not high enough to reach the terraces as yet!" he said. He seemed to take a childish delight in this annual battle with the sea despite the fact that it could only end in heavy financial outlay for him, whereas it cost the Atlantic nothing to attack us so savagely. Yet I understood, as Jolly did, the feeling of excitement the sight of the raging torrents of sea water gave Father. They excited us, too. That wild furious, relentless beating of the waves as they thundered forward and upward was awesome and exhilarating.

We were soaked through to the skin in the short minutes it took us to run from car to front door. Greg scooped me up in his arms as rain and salt spray drenched our hair and faces and carried me over the threshold. Jolly and Father stood dripping pools of water onto the hall floor, smiling at us.

"Better get out of our wet clothes" was all Father said.

Greg set me down, and without speaking we reached for each other's hands and went upstairs.

"I'll get tea on the go!" Jolly called after us.

We weren't thinking about tea as we opened the door to our room. The log fire was glowing with red embers, casting delicate golden shadows into the darkness. Greg went to the window and drew the curtains. This room and the bedroom had been decorated with new wallpaper — silver and white — and blue carpeting. The antique walnut furniture was a deep rich brown, and like the huge four-poster bed, very beautiful. Both bedspread and curtains were white velvet, and the whole effect was warm and softly welcoming.

Slowly, as if time had ceased to exist, Greg stripped off my dripping clothes as I stood in front of the fire. Strangely, I did not feel at all shy or self-conscious as I stood naked before him.

"You are very beautiful!" he told me, kneeling down in front of me and pressing his face against my body. I touched his wet fair hair, his face and neck, felt his desire as part of my own aching need of him.

He broke away from me and tore off his clothes with a sudden quick impatience. I smiled. His strong male body, was as beautiful to me as I hoped mine was to him.

When finally we lay on the carpet, limp and exhausted by our fierce hungry possession of one another, Greg touched my cheek and said softly:

"We should have used the bed, darling. And perhaps we should have waited a while."

A log split in two and sent a shower of sparks up the chimney.

"Oh, Greg," I whispered. "Nothing could have been more perfect!"

Everything was right. Time, place, and most of all Greg's lovemaking. I meant it and believed it was true. But when we loved each other a second time later that night, it was even more beautiful. This time we were not taking from each other but giving, and Greg was all that any woman could ask for in a lover.

"I wish I was older, wiser, more experienced!" I told him regretfully.

Greg kissed me.

"I should have hated it if you'd been

older, wiser, and more experienced. We'll learn about love together, my darling. It'll get better and better, I promise you."

Just for one second, on the brink of sleep, the thought shot across my mind: *He was not inexperienced!*

But I quickly put it out of my mind. Of course Greg and Jolly and any other young man of their age would have had some sexual experience. I wouldn't have expected otherwise. It would only have mattered if he'd ever loved another girl as much as he loved me.

Then I fell asleep. When we woke early on Christmas morning, Greg's arms were pulling me close to him, and as he kissed me, I thought that I could never feel such total happiness again.

We shared that Christmas day with Jolly and Aunt Tibby. Father went to sleep after the turkey, plum pudding, and brandy, so we left him quietly snoring in the library as we put on oilskins, sou'westers, and boots and trudged over to Trevellyan Hall. William, a sodden bundle of silky hair, scampered ahead of us. Greg never let go of my hand. I had the feeling he was half afraid he'd lose me if he did! But I was happy with this constant contact with him, and if Jolly felt like teasing us, he refrained from doing so. He seemed as anxious as Greg that nothing should spoil our happiness. I did not realize it at the time, but I know now that even then my brother did not trust his friend.

Aunt Tibby hugged Greg and kissed me, something she had never done in her life before. I thought I saw tears in her eyes as she gruffly congratulated me. But she was soon her normal brusque self as she informed Greg that a gentleman by the name of Mr. Richards had telephoned him from London and wished him to return the call as soon as he arrived.

I saw Greg's face as he received the news. His jaw clenched and his eyes closed for a moment as if he had received bad news. I was surprised, then told myself nothing mattered as long as it wasn't someone from the navy recalling Greg and Jolly from their Christmas leave.

"I'll phone back in a minute," Greg said, his voice so casual and disinterested that I forgot the mysterious Mr. Richards until after tea when I suddenly remembered that Greg hadn't yet made that call. I wondered why?

The reason became obvious later when Aunt Tibby suggested that since the rain had let up a little, we go to see the progress Pentyre had made to the stable flat.

"I'll join you in a few minutes," Greg said,

hanging back. "I'd better make that phone call now before I forget."

I knew then that he had been waiting for a chance to use the phone without Aunt Tibby, Jolly, and myself there to overhear him.

A good ten minutes elapsed before Greg joined us in the stables. He made no reference to the phone call, and I tried to put it out of my mind. I hoped he might mention it later on, but he did not do so. Eventually, sheer feminine curiosity got the better of me, and as we walked home to Tristan's Folly, I asked a casual question about Mr. Richards. Was he, I asked, a close friend of Greg's? Someone we should invite to our wedding reception when we finally fixed a date to have one?

"No, he's not a friend!" Greg replied, just a shade too sharply because Jolly then asked:

"Sounds as if he's bad news. Nothing wrong, Greg?"

"Nothing at all. Forget it!" Greg's voice was suddenly forbidding.

"Okay, don't bite my head off!" Jolly said, feigning defence against a flurry of physical blows. "You don't have to tell me to M.Y.O.B."

This, our childhood shortening of mind-your-own-business would normally have made Greg smile, but his face remained coldly impassive.

75

He was laughing again by the time we reached the house, and the mystery phone call was forgotten. I would probably have thought no more of it but for subsequent events. Then it was just another tiny piece of the vast, confused jigsaw of my relationship with Greg and his with the world.

There were no more incidents during that leave. For me they were wonderful, glowing, happy hours: the lull before the storm.

During our last night together Greg clung to me in a new and different way. It was as if he were the one in need of care and protection, I the older and wiser one who could make him feel secure.

"Swear you'll never stop loving me!" he kept begging me over and over again. "Promise you'll never leave me no matter what happens. I love you so much, Sammy. I couldn't live without you."

"Darling, don't even think about it!" I begged him. "How could I live without you? *Why* should we live without each other?"

He eased away from my encircling arms, and in the darkness I heard him laugh. It sounded false.

"I suppose I'm just too much in love with you."

When the final moment for parting came, he promised to write or phone me whenever he possibly could. I promised to write to him every day. He kissed me once more, and then he and Jolly were driving away as I had watched them do so many times before. My heart was at its lowest ebb, and tears were stinging my eyes. Father put his arm round me.

"Officers' wives don't cry!" he said. He patted my shoulder and added with a chuckle: "Though your mother always did, no matter how often I told her about the British stiff upper lip!"

I had a sudden longing then to talk to Father, really confide all my fears that Greg was not being entirely honest with me, that Jolly had spoken of a redheaded woman in Greg's life and I was afraid something quite serious might lie behind it. I wanted to ask Father whether, if Greg had been having an affair with her before he fell in love with me, she would have any grounds for blackmailing him?

But the mere thought struck me as dramatic and a little ridiculous, so I said nothing. I could not possibly doubt Greg's total love for me, and I convinced myself that was really all that mattered. I must do as I had promised and trust him. He would sort out his own affairs.

Father and I spent the evening discussing

the future. I did not want to leave him alone at Tristan's Folly, but he pointed out that he had become accustomed to my absence when I was living at the hospital and, in any case as Greg's wife, I ought to spend my off-duty days at Trevellyan Hall. I argued that if I did this, Aunt Tibby would almost certainly move to the stable flat, and I'd be alone at the Hall except on Greg's leaves.

"So I might as well stay here with you, Father," I finished.

In the end, we jointly devised what I felt to be a perfect plan. I would remain at Tristan's Folly with Father, Aunt Tibby would continue to live at the Hall, and when Greg had leave, he and I would use the stable flat. I couldn't wait to put this idea to Aunt Tibby, and so I telephoned her. She at once approved the plan. She would remain at the Hall until Greg and I wished to take up a more or less permanent abode there.

I suppose my Italian blood may make me emotional. Whatever the cause, I could not face Greg's and my big bed in the guest wing without him. That night I returned to my turret bedroom. It had not been altered since I was a little girl. My narrow brass bedstead still had the same patchwork quilt, the bookcase still held all the old nursery classics, the four narrow turret windows looking down to the sea still had the pink fringed blinds I could pull down after dark, blotting out the sight of the sea far below me.

I loved this room and spent many hours alone in it, sometimes writing at my small desk or curled up in the sprawling armchair, with its black and white panda cotton covers, reading a book. In the summer months I loved to sit on one of the four narrow window seats and watch the ships in the distance or throw stale bread to the wheeling gulls who came screaming down to catch the pieces in mid-air. A city child might have felt lonely in this room, but to me it was a familiar haven where I could dream away the hours undisturbed.

Nevertheless, as I climbed into my narrow bed, I was lonely, perhaps for the first time in my life, unbearably so without the comforting warmth of Greg's body against mine. I knew he was missing me every bit as much because he had telephoned from the wardroom to say good night and to tell me again how much he loved me.

My last thought before falling asleep was that I must keep my promise and trust him. I would not give the red-haired woman another thought. I could not prevent myself asking why Greg didn't trust me enough to tell me about her.

But I was asleep before an answer came to mind.

When the first exotic box of beautiful hothouse roses was delivered by a grinning boy, I was speechless with pleasure and excitement. The dark red roses lay in a cellophane box, tiny drops of water on the crimson velvet petals. The card said simply: '*With all my love, darling. Greg.*'

Father saw me arrange them. He smiled at me and aptly quoted Burns:

My love is like a red, red rose
That's newly sprung in June

But when, three days later, another box of flowers was delivered, Father frowned a little anxiously.

"Young Greg is being somewhat extravagant. I don't think he's that well off, is he?"

So on the phone that night I told Greg: "They are beautiful roses, darling, but I honestly don't want you to spend so much money on me."

Greg sounded hurt.

"Surely I can send you flowers if I feel like it?"

"But roses in January!" I persisted.

"I can afford them, darling. Believe me!" Greg said reassuringly.

I was, like any other young girl, touched, pleased, impressed. What could be more romantic than roses twice a week in midwinter? But Greg's generosity didn't stop at flowers. A case of champagne was sent up from the Saracen's Head with a message from Greg to say Father was to keep it in the cellar in readiness for the celebration party he wanted to give on his next leave.

"Can't think why he had it sent here," Father said as he told the delivery boy where to take the heavy case. "Why not have it sent to the Hall?"

I went to tea with Aunt Tibby. She, too, had been the recipient of a surprise present from Greg, a small but beautiful Persian rug.

"Greg says it's to go in the flat," Aunt Tibby told me. "He said that it would be nice for you two when you stay there, but it's really a present for me when I move out there for keeps."

We carried it to the new apartment. Pentyre had made a wonderful job of the conversion. The flat had two rooms and a kitchen and bathroom, all looking down on to the cobbled yard between the stable block and the house. He had pine-wood panelled the long, low sitting room and laid a pine block floor that, when it had been polished a few more times, would make a beautiful background for the new Persian rug.

"Greg always did have good taste," Aunt Tibby commented as we went back to the Hall. "Probably why he chose to marry you, Samantha."

It was the first real compliment she had ever paid me, and I was very happy that finally she was becoming my friend.

That afternoon, she talked more than I had ever heard her talk. She told me about Greg's father, a naval captain who had twice been decorated for gallantry before he was drowned at sea. I knew from old photographs that Greg greatly resembled him in appearance, though he had been even taller than Greg, a six foot seven giant of a man who had found it difficult to fit into a bunk at sea. He and Greg had the same crisp fair hair and fine features, and in all the photographs I saw he was laughing with that same wonderful look of joy I loved in Greg.

His mother was a more shadowy, less flamboyant figure. Aunt Tibby told me that she had been in very delicate health with a serious heart defect. She should not really have married let alone have a child. Like my mother, she had died in childbirth. Greg had never known her and seldom thought of her, Aunt Tibby having replaced her so competently.

In all the pictures I found Greg's mother beautiful. She had a pure oval face, like a Rossetti girl, with a classic, broad forehead and wide-spaced eyes, heavily lidded and long lashed. She had Greg's wide, generous mouth. Aunt Tibby told me, since none of the old photographs were coloured, that she had had auburn hair and hazel eyes.

Once or twice I felt Aunt Tibby was on the brink of talking about her engagement to Father. But although we came very near to it, at the last minute she shied away. I felt confident that one day soon that old wound would finally open, drain itself of bitterness, and heal. I hoped so both for her sake and Father's. One of the reasons I regretted the postponed wedding was that I was sure the church wedding would have brought them together. Aunt Tibby could not have refused to go to church.

Except for the brief excitement of Greg's letters and phone calls, life settled back into its quiet, uneventful serenity. Only the winter storms roused Tristan's Folly from its annual hibernation. I walked William, played chess with Father, knitted a sweater for Greg, and slowly began to put on weight. I paid my weekly visit to old Dr. Edwards, and he said I could soon think about going back to the hospital. I had a girl friend to stay for a weekend. I went to see her off at the station on Monday morning and was waving her good-bye, when quite without warning, I saw Greg.

I don't know whether I was more surprised to see *him* than I was to see the little red sports car he was driving as he pulled up with a screech of brakes.

"I nearly drove past without recognizing you!" he said as he pulled me into the car and hugged me. "Oh, darling, it's wonderful to see you. And we've a whole twenty-four hours together. A day and a night."

We drove somewhat dangerously up the hill to the Folly, Greg's arm around me, our voices continually breaking in on one another as we discussed the sudden unexpected chance to be together. It was not until we pulled up outside the front door that I found time to ask him about the car.

"Did you borrow it?" I asked. "It's terribly smart!"

Greg smiled.

"No, I didn't borrow it. I bought it. It's ours!" he announced. "Jolly's green with envy!"

He must have seen my puzzled expression.

He looked suddenly anxious.

"Don't tell me you don't like it!"

"Darling, of course I do. It's just that — well, it must have cost an awful lot of money."

Greg gave me a short, quick glance and turned away to get his suitcase from the back seat.

"So what? I've saved a bit. Why shouldn't I spend it now I have someone as beautiful, sweet, and attractive as you for a wife?"

I ought to have been pleased, but the compliment was too easy, too smooth. Father, when he saw the car, made suitable noises of appreciation, but just as I had done, he mentioned Greg's extravagance. I saw Greg's mouth tighten.

"I'm not exactly a pauper, sir," he said. "Even naval lieutenants get paid occasionally, you know!"

Both Father and I knew what a sub lieutenant earned. Jolly had frequently complained that his pay was woefully inadequate and usually succeeded in extracting a generous allowance from Father for what he termed 'a few luxuries.' This allowance paid for the insurance and upkeep of Jolly's second-hand car.

In our bedroom Greg looked defiant.

"I suppose you and your Father are going

85

to infer I've been extravagant again if I give you this."

He threw a small box carelessly onto the bed. He was obviously upset. I felt I had behaved churlishly and quite unfairly. If Greg had been frugally saving these past few years and now took pleasure in giving me things, it was hateful of me not to be thrilled and enthusiastic.

I grabbed the box and made much of hurriedly tearing off the wrappings. Inside lay a very beautiful heavy silver bracelet.

"Oh, Greg it's lovely!" I said, flinging my arms around him and hugging him. I let him fasten it on my wrist. He looked happier.

"I chose one with links because I want eventually to make it a charm bracelet," he told me almost shyly. "Wherever I go, and I suppose being in the navy I'll probably get to plenty of odd places around the world, I'm going to buy a special charm. Then, when we're very old and I've stopped my travels, we can sit in front of the fire and talk about each place and how much I longed for you when I was there without you."

"Oh, Greg!" I felt really regretful now at my earlier reactions.

He kissed me and then held me at arm's length, staring down into my face with serious concentration.

"It's from me to you," he said quietly.

The way he stressed the word 'me' puzzled me. It was as if he were saying that his other gifts were not personal as this one was. I did not know what to reply, so I just kissed him again, loving him with my whole heart.

Inevitably we caught fire from each other's lips and made love with a kind of desperate haste that left me, for the first time, a little incomplete. I doubt I could explain that feeling adequately. I was physically satisfied and yet mentally rejecting Greg's frantic urgency to possess me. It was almost as if he felt he had lost me and only now found me again.

That night he seemed a lot calmer, and I was happier as I fell asleep in his arms. I loved him so much, and knowing I had to be parted from him the next day lent a kind of agony to the joy. Perhaps, I thought, Greg had this same dread of separation. It would explain the desperate quality of his loving.

The following morning, despite the heavy rain, Greg insisted on taking me for a drive in his new car. We roared through the village High Street where quite a few heads turned to stare after us. Greg seemed determined to drive as fast as the little twisting Cornish roads would permit and with as much noise of revving engine as he could manage.

I came to the conclusion that I was really married to a little boy who wanted to show off his new toy and create an impression. I reminded myself that Greg, in comparison with Jolly, had been the 'poor relation.' If he wanted to show off a little now, it was only natural, and it would be cruel of me to spoil his fun.

All too soon it was time for him to leave. I felt terribly depressed and was only a trifle consoled by Greg's promise that he would try to arrange for me to spend a long weekend in Trenoun. I would have been so much happier if we could have had married quarters where I could live with him. But as Greg explained to me, he and Jolly were attached to a small training establishment where, since no one remained longer than eighteen months, married quarters did not exist.

As a naval officer's daughter, I knew very well what to expect when I married a naval officer, but I had not been able to imagine how hard it would be to endure these long separations from someone I loved. Now I told Father I wished Greg had become a doctor or dentist or even a coal man if it meant I could be sure he'd be home every evening after work.

Father looked suitably shocked. He referred to Greg's father.

"Old Rupert Trevellyan would turn in his grave if Greg had chosen any other career but the navy. Anyway, it's Greg's life. You know he and Jolly never considered any other."

"I know, I know!" I agreed testily. "But that doesn't stop me *wishing*!"

So Father softened and challenged me to a game of chess to take my mind off Greg's departure.

The next break in our quiet routine was a flying visit from Jolly. It was strange seeing him without Greg, for they usually managed to coincide leaves. This time, however, it seemed as if Jolly and Greg had deliberately opted for different days. I wondered if Jolly had been feeling 'odd man out' and if Greg and I had been tactless in showing our feelings so openly. We had held hands and kissed as if Jolly were not there. The last thing I wanted was to come between Jolly and Greg. That evening, when my brother came out to the kitchen to help me with the washing up, I told him so.

Jolly stacked some clean glasses on a tray and absentmindedly began to polish them a second time with his wet tea towel.

"Don't be silly! Of course you haven't come between us, idiot!"

He hesitated as if unsure whether to speak his mind. "But you are right about my wanting to take my leave separately. I wanted to talk to you alone, Sam, about Greg." He looked at me uneasily. "I'm a bit worried about him. He's been spending a hell of a lot of money lately. It isn't just the car. In the mess, too, he's always treating everybody to drinks as if he was made of money. He's got plenty of the ready on him, too. I don't understand it. Poor old Greg always had a bit of a job to make ends meet."

A soapy plate slipped out of my hands and splashed back into the water. Jolly's fears had revived my own.

"Greg explained things to me," I told my brother in what I hoped sounded a convincing tone of voice. "He said he wanted to splash out just for once in his life. He's using his savings."

Jolly shrugged his shoulders doubtfully.

"What savings? We never saved in our lives, Sam. As for splashing out, it isn't 'just for once'. He's been doing little else since Christmas."

Because I was so worried I was sharper than I intended when I said:

"It's Greg's business, not yours, what he chooses to do with his money."

Jolly disconcertingly ignored my unkind rebuke.

"I know it isn't my business, but in a way

it is yours, Sam, now you're married to him. I simply don't understand what he's up to. It's not just a little money he's throwing around. It's quite a lot. The other chaps have remarked on it, too. Word's going round that Greg must have come into a legacy. I suppose he hasn't, has he, Sam? That would explain everything. Could you ask Aunt Tibby, do you think?"

"I could, but I'm not going to," I replied. I was remembering suddenly my promise to trust Greg no matter what should transpire. I had not then understood why he had extracted my promise. Now I thought it could be this situation he had had in mind. "If Greg wants to explain everything to me, he will. If not, I'm not going behind his back to check up on him via Aunt Tibby."

Jolly did not argue. This was unlike him, and I ought to have known that his silence did not mean consent. Later that evening he went out in his car. Father and I thought he had gone down to the Saracen's Head for a drink. Actually he went to Trevellyan Hall. I was already in bed when he got back. He came straight to my room.

"Whether it's of interest or not," he told me, "Aunt Tibby told me tonight that no relative or friend of Greg's has died recently that she knows of, and certainly he's not been left any legacy or she'd have known about it."

I wished he had not forced the knowledge on me. I told him I was tired and wanted to sleep. But sleep eluded me. I knew that I had to have this out with Greg. It was not enough for me to trust him; he must also trust me. Somehow I felt the red-haired woman was involved in the mystery, but I was too cowardly to ask Jolly if Greg had been seen with her again. Moreover, I felt it would be just as disloyal to question Jolly as it would be questioning Aunt Tibby.

But nothing made sense. If the red-haired woman were blackmailing Greg (and that struck me as ridiculous and quite improbable), but *if* she were, he would be short of money, not the opposite. The only possible alternative to that idea was that she was giving him money. Could Greg be blackmailing her? That was so absurd, I surprised myself even thinking of it. I'd known Greg all my life, and I would have staked my life on his total integrity. It was as inviolate as mine or Father's or Jolly's.

Next morning there was yet another box of crimson roses from Greg. They gave me no pleasure at all. I put them in a vase in the hall and tried not to see them. I was like any silly ostrich putting its head in the sand.

5

The weather worsened, and the sea swept over the terraces and dragged back with its greedy green fingers the white wooden tubs that had housed my pink and scarlet geraniums throughout the summer. It also loosened several of the stones in the wall and left sand and pebbles strewn around the foot of the house in its wake.

"Going to be quite a battle this year by the look of it," Father said as he put on his oilskins and went out to repair the wall. I knew he was enjoying himself, but I couldn't enter into the spirit of what for him had now become an annual contest with the Atlantic. Move and countermove, I found myself beginning to hate the howl of the gale and the endless beating of the waves against the cliffside. I felt threatened and nervous. I became even more so when I saw William on the terrace one day nearly carried off by a gigantic wave. Obviously neither he nor Father had been expecting it. I ran to the door and shouted to the two of them to come indoors at once.

Father came in, a curiously speculative look on his face.

"Quieten down now, girl," he said, his voice steady and imperative. "No one's going to get hurt. See, William's enjoying it. Spaniels are water dogs, you know. They like getting wet, same way sailors do."

"They're not salt-water dogs!" I cried hysterically.

I had not realized I was so tense, but I was suddenly sobbing as though William had been swept away to a watery grave.

"Off you go and make some hot chocolate," Father ordered. "And put a tot of rum in it. In mine, too."

I felt a bit of an idiot as the quiet, warm atmosphere of the kitchen soothed my frayed nerves. Even more so when the small tot of rum in my cup made me sick. I wondered what was the matter with me. But I did not have to wonder for long. Father put through a call to Dr. Edwards, and when the old family physician came by that afternoon and asked me a few pertinent questions, I knew even before he told me that I was almost certainly pregnant.

"Well, be glad of it, girl!" the old doctor said, seeing the look of dismay on my face. "A child is the right way to bless a marriage. You and Greg should be proud of yourselves."

My first reaction of dismay changed suddenly to pleasure. I was carrying Greg's child, had a living part of Greg inside me that was mine to guard and hold. I'd never be lonely now, not even when he left me, I thought.

"She's much too young to be a mother," Father said gruffly, obviously shaken by the news. Dr. Edwards pooh-poohed that.

"The younger the better!" he said. "Healthier baby for one thing, easier birth for another, and a child early on in a marriage stops these youngsters becoming too self-centered."

I felt like laughing from sheer happiness. I'd never given a thought to having Greg's child. We were far too newly married to have discussed the possibility of a baby. But now it was certain, or almost certain. I was thrilled. I tried to remember the moment when I might have conceived. Dr. Edwards had given me a vague idea of the date, but I think I knew intuitively I had conceived that last beautiful time we made love during Greg's Christmas leave. We'd neither of us thought of being careful. We'd thought only of expressing our love for each other.

Father took Dr. Edwards to the library for a celebration drink. I stayed in my room to write to Greg. But I tore up the letter. I wanted to tell him in person so I could see his face express first his surprise, then his pleasure. I was wildly impatient to share the news with him. I almost told him that evening when he phoned, but I managed to control myself, saying only that I had something I very much wanted to discuss with him and asking him please, somehow, very soon, to arrange for us to be together.

But I had to wait a whole week before Greg was able to obtain a weekend leave.

Again Jolly did not accompany him. I was glad of this: I wanted to have Greg entirely to myself. I told him my news the moment we were alone together in our private sitting room. His reactions were almost the reverse of my own — first pleasure, then surprise, then disbelief, and finally dismay.

"It can't be true. *It just can't be!*"

I stared at him, bitterly disappointed by the way he had accepted my news.

"Dr. Edwards says it is definite, Greg. He took tests last week and confirmed yesterday that they were positive."

"I don't believe it!"

I realized Greg meant he didn't want to believe it. I longed to touch him, plead with him to want the baby, to be as thrilled as I was. But my pride and Greg's cold, dismayed face kept me at a distance. I was silent, waiting for him to digest the news, hoping that his reaction was just shock, that once he gave the matter some thought he would at least see how much *I* wanted the baby and be pleased for me, even if he couldn't be pleased about it himself. But he walked away to stare out of the window.

"Damn it!" he said at last. "*God damn it!*"

"Greg!" I was now the one who was deeply shocked. I had never anticipated such violence of feeling. Moreover, I felt superstitiously afraid of the way he had more or less cursed our child.

The sound of my horrified voice penetrated his mind. He turned and looked at me, his eyes narrowed and concerned.

"I'm sorry if I've upset you, darling," he said. "I didn't mean to. It's just that this *isn't* the right time for us to bring a child into the world."

The colour rose to my cheeks.

"Why not, Greg? What's wrong with *now*? I know it isn't a perfect world, but it never was, and it never will be, will it?"

"It's not that . . . " Greg's voice trailed off into silence.

"Then what is it? Perhaps I wouldn't feel

so hurt if I understood. Don't you *want* our child?"

Now he looked at me for the first time with warmth.

"Of *course* I do. But . . . well, *not now*, Sammy." He took a deep breath and looked away from me. I had the feeling that he was lying. "We've only just married. I want to have more time with you *all* to myself. Besides, we can't really afford a family yet."

I gave a scornful laugh.

"That's funny, coming from you. Or aren't babies as important as sports cars and flowers?"

"*Sammy, don't!*"

I knew I had hurt him, but I didn't care. I wanted him to feel as miserable as I did. He tried to put his arms around me. I twisted away from him and flung myself down on the sofa.

"I want the baby even if you don't," I said coldly. "So if you're thinking of asking me to get rid of it, it's pointless trying. I'd do anything in the world for you, Greg, but not that."

Now Greg was angry.

"You've no right to put words into my mouth!" He was furious. "Of course I wouldn't ask you to get rid of it. Be reasonable, darling. It's been a shock. I'm not in a position at the moment to add to my responsibilities. I suppose I really ought not to have married you in the first place."

Now he did frighten me. Was he regretting our marriage? I was appalled.

"I suppose I was weak," Greg continued, talking more to himself than to me. "But I loved you so much. I wanted you so badly."

"You sound as though your love and your need are things of the past."

He came to the sofa and sat down, his hands reaching out to frame my face. His expression was full of love and tenderness now. Yet he looked sad.

"Darling, I love you as much as I ever did, if not more," he said. "I want you desperately. Please believe that."

I think I did, but I held back.

"You have an extraordinary way of showing it, Greg." He nodded.

"I'm afraid that's true," he said in a tired voice. "But don't forget you made me a promise, darling. You said you'd keep faith with me no matter what. This is one of those occasions when you've just got to take me on trust. I do love you. I do want children with you. I just don't want a baby now, but don't ask me to give you reasons."

"It seems a funny way to begin a marriage!"

I said more calmly. "I know I promised to trust you, but I never thought it would mean we had to hide important things from each other. You *are* hiding something from me, aren't you, Greg? If you love me, and I believe you do, nothing that has happened to you in the past matters any more . . . not to me. I could forgive you anything, darling, however awful. Why can't *you* trust *me*?"

Instead of responding to this appeal, Greg got up and walked away from me. I'd lost him again. His voice became cold.

"Let's not go on with this, Sammy. I've nothing more to say. I'm sorry, but that's the way it is. I'm sorry, too, if my reactions about the baby upset you. I'll get used to the idea, no doubt, and in one way I am pleased. I hope it will be a little girl like you."

His words brought tears to my eyes. He must have heard me sniffing because he came hurrying back to me, and the next moment I was in his arms. As always when Greg became my lover, the problems that had worried or upset me were pushed to the back of my mind. I could think of nothing but the desire to be close to him again, secure in his arms and in his love.

Later we went together to break the news of my pregnancy to Aunt Tibby. Her delight compensated me a little for Greg's half-hearted acceptance of it. I think mainly for my sake he let Aunt Tibby believe he was as pleased as I was. Or, to be more accurate, as pleased as I had been. I could no longer feel the same degree of joy. I knew Greg did not really want the baby, and I thought of it now as something keeping us apart rather than bringing us closer together.

Aunt Tibby drew me into the kitchen before we left. I loved this vast room with its long scrubbed kitchen table and its old orange patterned curtains, the shabby rush matting on the stone floor, and the big stove that kept the room warm and cozy despite its size. It was here I had 'helped' Aunt Tibby make cakes and pastry when I was a little girl. I always felt at home in this room.

Aunt Tibby flicked an invisible crumb off the spotless tabletop and said:

"Don't you think it would be nicer for the baby if its parents were properly married?"

It was the nearest she could come to telling me outright that the child would seem illegitimate to her if we did not get our wedding blessed in church.

I smiled at her.

"I'd like the church ceremony very much myself. I'll talk to Greg about it," I promised.

But without understanding why, I found

myself reluctant to bring up the subject. I think I knew in my heart that Greg would not want it. A silly kind of pride made me want the suggestion to come from him. I dropped a few hints, but either Greg chose to ignore them or he truly didn't realize what was in my mind. Finally I said:

"Your Aunt Tibby has never reconciled herself to our registry-office wedding, Greg. You know what a staunch churchgoer she is. She more or less inferred she'd feel the baby was illegitimate if we didn't go to church to bless our marriage!"

Greg shrugged his shoulders.

"We're as legally married as we'll ever be, darling, and who's to say we aren't blessed? Aunt Tib's a bit old-fashioned."

I bit back the words: *Then so am I!* I said nothing, but the subject festered inside me and widened the growing rift between us. We seemed only to get really close to each other when we made love. Then it was as if Greg were once again the man I knew so well and loved so dearly. There were no secrets, no reservations, no evasions, no doubts about the way we loved one another. But inevitably, the aftermath of post-sexual content would give way to the now-familiar feeling that Greg was hiding something from me, that there was a barrier between us nonetheless real for being invisible.

After Greg had gone back to Trenoun, I wrote to the matron of the hospital in Newquay, explaining that I was pregnant and would therefore be unable to return to my training. I had a charming letter back from her, congratulating me, saying they would all miss me, as indeed they had already, and saying that my spell of training in the maternity ward would stand me in good stead!

I little thought as I read her kindly words that before long I would lie in that same ward having a miscarriage. For the present I was remarkably well and lucky enough to be one of those women who did not suffer from early-morning sickness. Despite Greg, I was happy to be carrying his child. I walked miles with William whenever the weather permitted. It was now late March. I knew spring was not far away, although there were still attacks from the sea when a gale blew it into a boiling cauldron, and it seemed bent on the destruction of Tristan's Folly.

One particularly mild afternoon Father and I took the bus to the hills of Trefarn Valley, one of the most beautiful parts of the countryside surrounding Tristan's Bay. We walked with William across soft green fields where the sheep had already given birth to their spring lambs. Here, instead of the seagull's cries, we listened to the larks singing and heard our first cuckoo. It was a gentler, softer landscape, with its lush meadows and tiny streams and budding hawthorn hedges. I felt calmer and less restless than I had felt of late on the headland.

Most afternoons I went to tea with Aunt Tibby. She had begun knitting for my baby. On one of those visits she told me that the mysterious Mr. Richards had phoned Greg again.

"I told him Greg was at Trenoun," she recounted, obviously puzzled. "But he didn't seem interested even when I tried to give him the telephone number of the officers' wardroom. He just wanted me to let Greg know immediately that he expected Greg to call back as soon as possible."

"But if it was urgent, surely it would be quicker for him to phone Trenoun?" I replied, perplexed.

Aunt Tibby nodded over her knitting.

"That's what I thought. Very odd! But I popped a letter in the post to Greg, and that was that."

"You don't know who this Mr. Richards is?"

Aunt Tibby shook her head.

"I haven't any idea," she said. "I didn't

know Greg had any friends in London. There is a solicitor in Lincoln's Inn who handled his father's estate, but his name is Garson. Perhaps it's someone from Mr. Garson's office. Or maybe one of Greg's old school friends."

But Jolly knew all Greg's school chums, and if it had been one of them, Mr. Richards would surely have identified himself by giving his first name as well as his last, or would perhaps have asked after Jolly. I puzzled over it all. It was possible, I supposed, that it was someone from the firm who handled Greg's legal affairs. Momentarily I settled for this possibility and forgot the matter again.

When I arrived home, Father informed me that I had had a visitor.

"A man from Welfare, whatever that is!" he told me. "Wanted all kinds of information about you and Greg. I told him he'd better come back tomorrow."

I presumed, like Father, that this was part of the Health Service, although I had not notified anyone that I wanted to claim maternity benefits or made inquiries about grants or baby clinics. It seemed too soon for that, especially as I had not yet felt the baby move inside me. But as Dr. Edwards might quite well have notified the authorities as a matter of routine, I gave my visitor no thought until two days passed without a second Welfare visit. Then I questioned Father more closely. He tried to describe the man to me.

"I suppose he was middle-aged, going grey. Wore what I'd call a London suit — noticed the cloth, come to think of it. Crossed my mind someone wasn't doing so badly out of the National Health!"

"But didn't he give any name or say where he came from?" I asked.

Father looked at me over the top of his glasses.

"I don't think he did — just said he came from Welfare. Never asked the fellow his name. Thought he looked like a well-dressed tax inspector.

I smiled, knowing Father's dislike of tax officials.

"But what exactly did he want to know?" I persisted. "What kind of questions did he ask?"

"How often Greg got leave; if I thought you seemed happy together. That kind of thing. I thought it was a bit impertinent. Nearly told him to mind his own business. Then he had the nerve to ask me if Greg had a private income. I told him outright he'd better ask Greg because that was not my business." Father chuckled. "It must have been obvious I didn't think it was any of his business, either! Anyway, he left, and that was that."

Knowing Father's antipathy to any kind of encroachment on what he termed 'personal liberty,' to the point of being obsessional on the subject when forms arrived to be filled in requesting his age or details of his private life, I thought at first that he had probably misjudged the poor man whose job it was to help me and my baby. But a few days later, when I went to Dr. Edwards' office for my checkup, I was staggered when he told me it was about time I notified the authorities I was pregnant.

"But haven't you already done that?" I asked. "Someone from Welfare came to see me last week, so I assumed you had told them."

"From Welfare?" The old man stared at me. "The only person likely to call on you, my dear, would be the Health Visitor and then not until your baby was born. They've got far too much to do to go visiting healthy young patients like you. You're not counted an invalid, you know, just because you're having a baby. Why not walk to the clinic on Thursday. Do you a power of good!"

I went home to tell Father he must have been mistaken. According to Dr. Edwards there wasn't even a government department called Welfare.

Father was quite annoyed.

"Don't you try making me out to be in my dotage!" he said testily. "I may be retired, but I'm not senile. Of course the fellow came from Welfare. Or said he did."

"I expect there's an explanation somewhere," I said, and dropped the subject. I half believed there was a logical explanation, that Father's visitor would turn up one afternoon, and I'd discover he was doing some sort of census or market research for baby foods! I mentioned it to Greg in one of my letters only because I had no other news. Greg's reply came by return mail.

If that man calls again, you're to tell me (at once) . . . I agree with your father absolutely, that no one has a right to pry into our private lives. Don't let anyone like that into the house, darling. After all, it could be a potential burglar sizing up the place. Please be careful!

I don't know why, but the suggestion of a possible burglar seemed to come as an afterthought, a joke. I had the feeling that Greg didn't really think our strange visitor was a burglar, either. Whoever he was, however, the man did not call again, and Greg seemed very relieved when I went to Trenoun for the long delayed weekend and we had a chance to talk about it.

Greg booked me into a quiet hotel overlooking the harbour. It had been built only a few years ago and had a small garden at the back with steps leading down to the jetty. It was very comfortable and seemed to me to be occupied mostly by tourists. I had expected the place to be filled with Wrens and sailors, but during my brief stay there I never saw one uniform. Nor did Greg invite any of his friends to come and meet me.

"I hope you won't think me selfish, darling," he said in answer to my query about this, "but I specially chose this hotel because I want you all to myself. One can have enough even of the navy, you know!"

Newly married and in love though I was, I had led a terribly restricted, quiet life at home for the past six months. I had been looking forward to a little gaiety. I'd thought Greg might take me out to dinner and to dance, perhaps and even throw a little party to introduce me to his friends. Perhaps Greg had expected to see me looking obviously pregnant and had not wished to 'show me off' in that condition. In fact, the baby was barely noticeable except for a slight rounding of my normally flat stomach.

"You're beautiful!" Greg told me that first night. "More beautiful than ever, darling."

I know he meant it. Just as I know he meant it when he laid his head against my body and said: "We created our child out of absolute love, didn't we, darling?"

We were very, very close that night. I felt that Greg had suddenly become reconciled to the idea of fatherhood and that he had begun to feel a genuine affection for the baby I was carrying. I was very happy. But it was a precarious happiness. I ought to have realized that it could not last. It crumbled the moment Jolly walked through the hotel door.

6

It was afternoon, and it was raining. Greg and I were in the hotel lounge making the best of the bad weather, sipping tea in front of a good fire.

"Hullo, Sam!" Jolly's voice startled us both. He smiled down at me. "Any tea left?" he asked, helping himself to one of the sandwiches on my plate.

I did not notice immediately that he was talking only to me as he sat down beside me. It seemed natural enough that he should be asking me questions about Father and William and how the house was standing up to the storms. It was only when I turned to offer Greg another cup of tea that I realized Jolly had neither glanced at him nor spoken to him. Greg might have been a total stranger. I tried to draw him into the conversation, but Greg refusing a second cup of tea, stood up abruptly and said to me:

"You and Jolly must have lots to talk about. I'm going out for a walk. It's stuffy in here."

"But, Greg . . . " I began when I felt

Jolly's foot kicking mine under the table. As I watched Greg walk out of the room, I heard Jolly say quietly:

"Let him go, Sam!"

I looked at him uncomprehendingly.

"What is it? What's wrong?" I asked. "You two haven't quarrelled, have you?"

I was shocked to see the bitterness in my brother's face. He no longer looked like the brother I knew, but tired, lined, dejected and bitter.

"One can't quarrel with Greg," he said quietly. "He won't fight back."

"I don't understand. Why should you want to quarrel with him? Why do you want him to fight back?"

Jolly seemed to be having difficulty in answering. I saw him literally struggling for words, his face unutterably miserable. His obvious embarrassment had the effect of calming me.

"Jolly, whatever it is that has happened, you've got to tell me." I had a sudden flash of insight. "That's what you came here to do this afternoon, isn't it? But you're torn between loyalty to Greg and loyalty to me. I understand that, but you wouldn't have made up your mind to come here if you hadn't believed it was the right thing to do. So out with it, Jolly, whatever it is."

Jolly still hesitated. When he spoke it was to ask:

"You love Greg very much, don't you?"

"You know I do!"

"And so do I, damn it!" Jolly's voice broke. "That's what beats me, Sam. We've been friends all our lives. I'd have trusted him with my life and expected him to trust me with his. *Yet he refuses to explain.* I simply don't understand."

"Explain *what*, Jolly?"

He turned then and with an uncharacteristic gesture took my hand and held it tightly.

"I told Greg I was going to talk to you if he wouldn't offer me a reasonable explanation. I begged him to do so. But he just clamped his mouth shut and told me to do my worst."

"Then do it!" I said sharply. "I don't think anything you could tell me will stop me loving Greg. So it isn't all that vital, is it? But if something is wrong, then if I know about it, perhaps I can help to put it right."

"That's what I hope." Jolly let the words out in a rush.

"For weeks I've worried, wondering if you'd be happier left in ignorance. But Sam, *Greg is still seeing her.* He doesn't even take the trouble to hide it from me. You'd think he'd be ashamed; or at least

113

have some finer feelings in the matter. It's almost as if he *wanted* me to know."

"Her? The redhead?"

Jolly nodded. I let out my breath. Now at least I knew what I was up against. But I still couldn't quite believe it. Greg loved me. I know he did. Last night I did not — could not have — entertained a single doubt.

"All the other officers know what's going on," Jolly continued relentlessly. "They pretend not to because they know you're my sister. When I go into the wardroom they stop discussing Greg's affair. I've told Greg they all know, but he doesn't seem to care. He just tells me to mind my own business."

"Jolly, do *you* know who she is?"

He shook his head.

"I saw her once, accidentally. I stopped in at the bar of the Carlton for a drink late one evening on my way home. I saw her sitting in an alcove with Greg. She's quite a bit older than he is, thirty-fivish, I'd say. Nicely dressed. Sophisticated. Well-off, I think."

"Attractive?"

I was punishing myself, but I had to know. "Very!"

So that was it. The 'older woman', the mistress, maybe, who still had a hold on him.

"Not Greg!" I whispered.

"I know!" Jolly said miserably. "I still can't reconcile his behaviour with the Greg we know. Oh, he and I used to fool around with girls in the old days; we had the odd night here and there, but as far as I know, and I should know, Greg never had a serious affair. We were just fooling around," he repeated. "This woman — well, his interest in her seems to have started since he married you. That's what I *don't* understand."

"The fact that you saw them together one evening . . . "

"It's every fortnight," Jolly broke in ruthlessly.

"Every fortnight then," I said in such a matter-of-fact voice it did not sound like mine at all. "That doesn't prove Greg is having an affair with her. Having a drink with a woman doesn't necessarily mean an affair."

"Then why doesn't Greg talk about her if they're just 'good friends'? If the association is innocent? Why hasn't he told you about her? Why doesn't he put the record straight in the wardroom? He knows everyone thinks she's his mistress."

I thought suddenly of Greg's words: "Trust me, no matter what happens!"

It seemed now that he had known the

day he married me that I'd find out about this woman one day and had been trying to protect himself. But why? It would have been so much easier, and more honest, if he'd told me the truth at once even if he had to admit he'd had a mistress he was finding difficult to discard. Maybe he had tried to put her out of his life before we were married. That would explain why he had postponed the first wedding date. Nevertheless, it had been Greg who had rushed us to the registry office at Christmas. Had that been a desperate measure to make this woman understand that the affair was all over? Perhaps it had not succeeded. Was she holding something over him? But what? In any case, once he told me the facts, there'd be no further opportunity for blackmail. If she *was* blackmailing him . . .

My mind twisted and turned like a rat in a trap. Only Greg could provide the answers. But according to Jolly, he would not. Not only was Greg jeopardizing his marriage, but also his career. The navy was still old-fashioned about its officers behaving in blatantly immoral ways. Greg wasn't even being discreet. It was irresponsible, insane.

Jolly said:

"I'm sorry to spoil your weekend like this, Sam. I hope I've done the right thing telling

116

you. It isn't just because I'm worried for you. I'm concerned for Greg's career, too."

I gave Jolly's hand a reassuring squeeze.

"I know you love him, too," I said.

He nodded and stood up.

"Greg will be back soon, and I don't want to be around when he does. Call me if you need help, *any* sort of help, Sam. Okay?"

After he left, I went upstairs to our room and waited for Greg. It was a full hour before he returned, and when he did he looked strained and tired. I wanted to run to him and put my arms round him, but I could not.

He studied me, then said without emotion:

"I see Jolly's spilled the beans!"

"You knew he was going to do that." I defended my brother.

"He was doing what he thought best," Greg admitted without rancour.

"But, Greg ... " I steadied my rising voice and tried again. "Greg, what I don't understand is why you didn't tell me yourself."

"Yes, well ... " He said vaguely, moving away to the dressing table so that he no longer faced me.

"Greg, like it or not, I am your wife. Don't you agree that this is an impossible situation for me? What am I supposed to think? What

117

am I supposed to do?"

"Just trust me!"

I felt exasperated. What had he done so far to justify my trust?

"At least will you tell me who this woman is? What she means to you? Do you love her?"

"Of course not!"

His reply was so instantaneous and matter-of-fact that I believed him.

"What is she to you that you'll put your marriage and your career at risk?" I went across the room to him then and took hold of his arms and forced him to look at me. "Greg, even if *I* take you on trust, what about your superiors? Your career?"

Greg's jaw stiffened.

"My senior officers know about it . . . or rather, they think they do. I've already been told I shall be bypassed for promotion."

I was shocked.

"But why?" I asked. "If she's just a friend . . . ?"

"She's a married woman — the wife of an army officer," Greg said harshly.

"*Married!*" Somehow I had never thought of her as a married woman. That seemed to make matters worse. I tried to readjust my thinking.

"Do you mean you were in love with this

woman but couldn't marry her because she already had a husband? Then you married me hoping it would put an end to the relationship? Is that what happened?"

Surprising me yet again, Greg actually laughed.

"Of all the wild notions, Sammy!"

I was suddenly very angry with him, most of all for making me sound ridiculous.

"If my ideas are so wayout, whose fault is it?" My voice was rising but now I didn't care. "If you told me what was really happening, I wouldn't have to make such wild suggestions, would I?"

"No, you're right; I apologize," Greg said, still infuriatingly calm.

"Then tell me and stop being so cruel!" I shouted. "I've a right to know!"

Greg gave me a long look I can only describe as sad.

"I can't!" he said. "You've just got to leave me to sort things out by myself."

I continued to rail at him, to plead for over an hour. I accused him of lack of consideration, of cruelty, of avoiding the truth, all of which he freely admitted. But at the end of each attack he still refused to enlighten me further.

"How can I go on trusting you under these circumstances?" I finally asked him, exhausted both physically and emotionally. "You've no right to ask me to do so."

Greg nodded, his gaze stonily focused on a picture of a sailing ship on the wall.

"I know. But I love you, and you love me. I *am* asking you to go on believing in me, not as a right but as a hope. If the situation is too much for you and you find it intolerable, then naturally I won't stand in your way if you want to divorce me."

"Divorce you!" I echoed stupidly. Such a thing had not occurred to me. I felt sick with fear. "Greg, have I one good reason for divorcing you?"

He drew in his breath.

"If you mean, have I been unfaithful to you, no, I haven't."

"Have you ever wanted to be?" I suddenly knew that this was much more important. I was beginning to grow up.

"No!" was Greg's reply.

I made one last attempt to reach the truth.

"If you can't tell me, why can't you confide in Jolly?" I pleaded with him. "You know he would help you."

"I don't need Jolly's help!" Greg snapped out the words.

Hope died in me. I gave up. I felt drained and dreadfully unhappy. Greg looked even more so. His face was drawn, and he might have been ten years older than his age. I tried to introduce a more normal domestic note between us.

"Greg, I'm going to run a bath for you. Then we can go down to dinner," I said. Nothing much mattered at this moment except bringing back that gentle curve to Greg's beloved mouth and a smile to his eyes.

He responded at once to my softened approach. By mutual consent we made no further reference during dinner to Greg's affairs. Our conversation, a little strained on both sides, related entirely to Father, Aunt Tibby, William, and our respective homes. Those seemed to be the only safe topics.

I was thoroughly uneasy when we finally made our way upstairs to our bedroom. I wondered if Greg would want to make love to me, and if so, how we could possibly lie in each other's arms with such a vast gulf of misunderstanding between us. How could I give myself to my husband mentally or physically when we both knew that he was not prepared to give himself to me in the same way?

Greg, always acutely sensitive as a lover, made no approaches after he had climbed into bed beside me. We lay in the darkness, not quite touching one another, silent and miserable. I was the one who weakened. I was afraid that because I had to leave him and go home the next day, this horrifying gulf between us would continue to widen. I needed desperately the reassurance of his love. If I had that, I told myself, I could bear anything. So I reached out for his hand and put it against my breast.

I heard him draw in his breath. For a single moment I thought he was not going to gather me into the usual passionate embrace. Then his lips came down on my mouth in a fierce hunger that momentarily frightened me.

Neither of us spoke as we clung feverishly to one another, seeking a unity that both of us knew in our hearts was impossible in the circumstances. We were using our bodies and our physical hunger for each other as an escape. I hated him for being the cause of this emotional separateness. Yet my body was responding to his demands. All too soon we were lying exhausted but not really satisfied.

Greg kissed me good night. He must have tasted the salt tears that trickled down my cheeks, but he said nothing. I tried to comfort myself with the memory of our lovemaking, with the tenderness of that last kiss. But I knew, with a terrible painful awareness, that sex had solved nothing for us. And by his silence I knew Greg was aware of it, too.

7

I tried not to brood as the train chugged its way back to Newquay. But try as I might to put such thoughts out of my mind, I kept remembering everything Jolly had told me and was tormented by Greg's refusal to explain or justify himself.

I relived the misery of our last night together. At the bus terminal where I had half an hour to wait for my bus connection to Tristan's Bay, I tried to bury myself in an old book I had found in a shop in Trenoun, the famous story of 'Tristan and Isolde'. I knew the legend, and it fascinated me. From my early teens I had read and re-read the story of the tragic lovers. Father had once driven me through Tintagel, and we had gone into King Arthur's Castle Hotel to see the huge Round Table inscribed with the names of the knights. It was supposed to be a copy of the original. Nobody knows if it is fact or fiction, but it was said that King Arthur of Cornwall had sent abroad his trusted knight, Tristan, to bring back the Lady Isolde, who was to be his queen. They had returned together by ship and had fallen in love.

But Isolde was pure and Tristan a man of great integrity, devoted to his King, so they resolved to remain loyal, lying together but keeping Tristan's sword between them. Then Isolde's old nurse put a love potion in their wine, and after drinking it, Tristan and Isolde became lovers. When eventually the King discovered that Tristan had betrayed him, Tristan was killed on these sands in Cornwall in a terrible duel.

Today I felt particularly sad for the legendary lovers and for myself because there was a shadow hanging over Greg and me. And as I looked at the rain sweeping in from the sea, even the sky was weeping, I thought wretchedly.

Then suddenly the bus skidded on the narrow wet road. The book fell from my hands. The bus careered into a stone wall. I was flung forward, and my head crashed against the seat in front of me.

I recovered consciousness briefly in the ambulance that took me to Newquay Hospital. In a dazed way I recognized the face of the ambulance attendant who sat beside me.

"It's John, isn't it?" I muttered. Then a wave of darkness and pain pushed me back into oblivion.

Somewhere far back into the realms of my

subconscious, I heard a siren screaming. But I did not know the urgency was for me.

The next forty-eight hours remain a hazy confusion of pain and shadowy dreams. I was vaguely aware that at some time Father was by my bed, holding my hand, that my former friend, Peggy, was nursing me, and that I was in a hospital. Mostly I was aware only of sickness and pain.

I woke to full consciousness to find Greg beside me. When I first opened my eyes, he was looking away from me, so I was able to study him. I tried very hard but could not quite succeed in remembering when I had last seen him. His face was indescribably dear to me, yet different. He looked so sad.

I lay there drowsy and content, no pain now, thinking how much I loved him. I thought, too, about my oldest memory of loving him. He was a very little boy up in the apple tree in the garden at Trevellyan Hall. He was eating an apple and laughing down at me. I suddenly felt a great longing to have a little boy just like him, with thick unruly fair hair and laughing sailor's eyes.

"I hope it's a boy," I said dreamily.

Greg turned at the sound of my voice. I was shocked to see tears in his eyes.

"Darling Greg!" My voice was so weak

I had to repeat the words. They sounded far away.

Then Greg's arms went around me. I was surprised to feel the wetness of his cheek as he laid it against mine and said:

"I love you, I love you, I *love you!*"

"I love you, too!" I whispered weakly but cheerfully.

Peggy came in, grinned at us now lying on the bed together, and went out again saying:

"Better not let Sister see you. She'll be 'round presently."

"We're in hospital, aren't we?" I asked him. "Why? Have I been ill?"

He brushed his hand across his eyes and sat up holding my hand very tightly.

"You were in a bus that skidded and hit a wall," he told me. "You're a bit concussed, darling, but you're getting better now."

I remembered the bus ride, the dark wet roadway, and the grey stone wall. I remembered that I was on my way home from Trenoun and had been thinking about Greg and myself and the future.

"Greg, the baby. It's all right?"

I waited for his reassuring affirmative, but it didn't come. He merely held my hand more tightly. With my free hand I felt my body beneath the bedclothes. I knew then that I had lost the baby. I looked at Greg's face, hoping that he would deny it, but he could not.

I was still weeping quietly into my pillow when Sister came in. Greg was trying helplessly to comfort me, but she quickly sent him out of the room and called Peggy in to give me an injection.

I tried not to wake up again. But I was young and strong and much more resilient than I guessed. Within a week I was home with Father, a little weak but recuperating steadily — physically, if not mentally. I'd not seen Greg again since that day in hospital, and strangely enough I did not want to. Although at the time he had seemed genuinely sorry about the lost baby, I now felt that he had only been sorry for me. He had not wanted a child in the first place, and I was certain that he was relieved we wouldn't be having one after all. His daily letters were filled with love and concern but left me devoid of emotion. I existed in a vacuum and felt nothing at all.

Aunt Tibby told me this numbness was a form of self-protection and would wear off. She knew all about it, she said. And for the first time ever, she spoke freely of the day Father had jilted her.

"I bottled up my feelings so securely I

felt quite numb," she said. "There they stayed, quietly festering, slowly turning me into a bitter old woman who was wasting her life hating someone who really did not deserve such hatred. It would have been very wrong of your father to go through with the wedding once he knew he had fallen in love with another woman. I know it now, but I didn't, couldn't, accept it then. So don't let bitterness spoil your life, Samantha. Greg may not have felt ready for fatherhood, but that doesn't make him glad you lost your baby. I know he regrets it deeply. He told me so, as I'm sure he has told you."

I tried to accept the situation. But I was dreadfully depressed, so that the slightest upset would reduce me to tears. Father was worried. He must have written to Greg about me because Greg got compassionate leave and came home for a week.

Our relationship remained awkward and strained. I did not know if he was continuing his fortnightly meetings with the woman Jolly had described but whose name I still did not know. I told myself that if Greg really loved me, he would have wanted to relieve my mind of every worry, that the least he could do would be to explain the mysterious way he had been behaving.

He was gentle, tender, loving. But I

could not respond. I felt cold, withdrawn, unapproachable. I wasn't prepared to meet him on his terms, only on my own. And Greg would not talk. We shared the same big four-poster bed in the guest wing; we even made love, but it was never satisfactory for either of us, and I think Greg was as miserable as I, although he hid it better than I could. We both retreated into ourselves and spoke little to each other unless we were with other people. We didn't want to let Father or Aunt Tibby see the ever-widening rift between us.

Matters might have stayed in this strange limbo for the remainder of Greg's leave had it not been for another phone call from Mr. Richards. This time he phoned our house and not Trevellyan Hall. Unfortunately for Greg, I answered the call in the library a minute or two before Greg picked up the receiver on the upstairs extension.

"It's okay, Sammy. The call's for me," I heard his voice break in on Mr. Richards' request to speak to him. "If you put your receiver down, I'll take the call up here."

I replaced the receiver at once and stood staring down at it. I was no longer numb but seething with curiosity; with resentment at Greg's secretiveness; with that unaccountable sense of foreboding the earlier call had evoked in me.

It was only a matter of minutes, if not seconds, before I heard the faint tinkle as Greg replaced his receiver. It had been a remarkably short call.

I waited for Greg to come downstairs. He had gone up to our room to fetch a thick sweater, and he intended to take William for a long walk across the sands. But when he did not reappear, I decided to go up and see what had delayed him.

Far from going for a walk, he was sitting at the desk in our sitting room writing in a small notebook. As I entered the room and approached him, he snapped it shut so that I was in no doubt he wished to prevent my seeing what he was writing. Anger took over from curiosity.

"Did you think I was going to try to spy out your nasty little secrets?" The cold bitterness of my voice surprised me and brought an instant reaction from Greg. I may have been wrong, but I took his expression for fear. His voice, however, was as angry and bitter as my own as he snapped back:

"You have done little else but attempt to pry into my private affairs, Sammy, so you can hardly blame me for taking adequate precautions."

131

I was shocked into silence. My curiosity was natural and excusable. Of course I expected my husband to tell me about his friends, his activities when I was not with him. Just as it would have been perfectly natural for Greg to ask what I did when he was not around. Married couples, I had believed, did not have 'private affairs'. I regained my composure but I did not hesitate to tell Greg what I thought of his behaviour.

His expression changed from anger to exasperation.

"You seem to forget, Sammy, that I warned you *before* we were married there were some things I couldn't talk about. You agreed to trust me. You promised. It is not my fault if you cannot keep that promise."

I *had* promised. But I had no inkling then how far Greg would stretch that faith. Or for how long.

Steadying myself, I tried to compromise.

"Can't you at least give me a date in the future when you can explain what's happening? If you did that, I might find it easier to cope with everything now," I said quietly. "This mystery has been going on so long, Greg. How much longer before you can confide in me? Weeks, months?"

I waited for his reply, but when it came, it was a bitter blow to me.

"I simply cannot satisfy your curiosity, Sammy. Sorry, but I *can't*."

I spoke angrily again.

"You mean this could go on for years?"

He looked away from me.

"Possibly!"

"Well, I'm not waiting years!" I cried. Now the numbness that had really only concealed the unhappiness inside me gave way to a rush of violent emotion I could not stem. "This isn't a real marriage at all! If you loved me, you'd trust me the way you expect me to trust you. You don't love me. I'm beginning to doubt you ever did. You just married me so you would have a licence to enjoy making love to me whenever you couldn't make love to your other woman. Obviously one isn't enough for you. Well, now you're going to have to choose, Greg Trevellyan. And to make it easier for you, I'll choose for you. You can have her. *I* don't want *you* any more."

Perhaps if Greg had stood up and taken me in his arms and sworn his love for me, his willingness never to see the red-haired woman again, I would have burst into tears and told him I didn't really mean any of my furious words. But he stayed perfectly still.

Only the trembling of his hands betrayed any emotion at all.

"I've never been unfaithful to you, Sammy, or wanted to be. I married you because I loved you. I know now it was wrong of me to do so. All I can say is forgive me."

I wanted so much to believe him. My whole body ached with the desire to be reconciled with him. I made one last feeble attempt at a compromise.

"You mean you're sorry because I won't take you on crazy blind trust. Well, I won't, Greg; not unless you trust me. Just explain who this Mr. Richards is. I won't insist you talk about 'your woman'."

Greg's mouth tightened.

"She isn't 'my woman' and as far as Richards is concerned, I can only tell you he is an acquaintance."

"In other words, you won't tell me anything. You don't trust me any more than I trust you, and that makes a perfect marriage, doesn't it!" My sarcasm was biting. "About the only subject we can discuss freely and openly is sex. Well, I don't want that sort of marriage. If you've nothing to share with me but your body, you can keep that to yourself, too."

Furious, crying, I gathered up as many of my clothes as I could see through my tears and rushed out of the room.

In my own room, I dumped my belongings on my bed and threw myself on top of them. My tears broke into gulping sobs. I was filled with self-pity. And I hated Greg now with the same intensity as I had once loved him.

But hate and love are opposite sides of the same coin, and when I heard Greg's footsteps on his way downstairs, I stopped crying and listened. He went into the library to see Father. I could hear their voices. Then I heard Greg go out of the front door, William whining so miserably I knew Greg had not taken him for a walk. Seconds later, I heard the car engine — Greg was actually leaving! *And I didn't want him to leave.* I ran to my window and saw the rear lights of the red sports car disappearing down the drive.

I was still standing there when there was a knock on my bedroom door. It was Father. He looked old and anxious.

"Greg's returned to Trenoun," he said, and coughed, avoiding my gaze. "He tells me you two have had a tiff, and he thinks it will be better for both of you not to be together for a while."

"A *tiff*! Is that what he calls it? Oh, Daddy!" I rushed into his arms and sobbed against his shoulder. "It's worse than that! We had a row — a real one. I told Greg I

135

didn't love him anymore, but I didn't really mean it. I mean, I did mean it when I said it, but not *really*."

Father patted my head and gave me his handkerchief, then sat me down on the bed. He sat in the chair beside me and took out his pipe and slowly lit it. When it was going to his satisfaction, he said:

"Care to tell me about it? You don't have to if you don't want to, darling. But if it would help . . . " He paused, puffing out the familiar smoke.

I took a deep breath and tried to smile.

"I don't know if I can. I mean, it's all so *silly*!"

"It usually is. Young people are so intense. Suppose I was, too, when I was your age. Things matter too much then."

"Did Greg tell you anything? Anything at all?" I asked.

Father shook his head.

"Only that you'd had this tiff and that you were upset and, he thought, perhaps still not one hundred per cent fit after your miscarriage. He asked me to explain and to look after you."

"I see!"

"So long as you do you can't regard it as a tragedy, darling. Cheer up, will you?"

I gave him a watery smile.

"But I don't really understand anything at all, Father!"

Suddenly I was telling him all my forebodings, of Greg's strange behaviour, Jolly's warnings, the promise Greg had extracted from me — everything that had brought Greg and me to this state. Father listened without interruption. When I concluded my story, he was frowning and clearly perplexed.

"It all sounds so totally unlike Greg!" he said finally. "Quite out of character. He was always such an open, honest chap. And I'd stake my life on his integrity. Can't imagine him sneaking around, behaving badly behind people's backs. Must be a mistake somewhere."

I knew what Father meant, but I had to reiterate.

"Jolly wouldn't lie about such things. And Greg did not deny he was meeting this woman."

Father now began to look as unhappy as I felt.

"The boy ought to speak out!" he said. "Give an account of himself. Want me to talk to him, Sammy?"

"Yes, if I thought it would do any good. But if he won't tell *me*, and we've been so close, Father . . . " my voice broke.

137

"Yes, well, don't treat this as the end of the world!" Father said quickly. "I suppose we've just got to take Greg on trust. You promised, so don't go back on that now, Sam, just because the going's a bit tough. It was, of course, a silly promise to make in the first place, though you weren't to know it. But having made it, you've really got to stand by it, haven't you?"

It was just like Father to stick rigidly to what was fair and just.

I told him I felt that if Greg claimed the right to keep a serious secret from me, I in turn could claim the right to keep a part of myself from him. I wasn't prepared, I told Father adamantly, to be a real wife to Greg until he was prepared to be a real husband to me.

Father looked doubtful.

"I'm not sure you aren't becoming a bit confused, Sam. But that's a decision only you can make for yourself. All I'm saying is that you hurt a man's pride in a very particular way if you tell him his lovemaking is unwelcome, no matter what reason you imagine you have. I might also add, on a more practical level, that if there *is* another woman in the picture, you'd be doing yourself a disservice by leaving her the field. Not good tactics at all. Never give the enemy the advantage."

Despite the seriousness of our conversation, I had to smile at Father's professional summing up.

He leaned forward and patted my head.

"It will sort itself out, you'll see," he said. "Now dry those tears and come downstairs. You haven't given me a game of chess all week, what with Greg being home to monopolize you."

As he had known it would, the game took my mind off my immediate problem. But later that night, when there was no phone call from Greg, and pride had prevented me from phoning him, I was again in tears as I climbed into my lonely bed, not knowing how long it would be before I felt his arms around me again.

I woke to hear a crash like thunder and a fiendish rattling at my turret windows.

I switched on my bedside lamp, sprang out of bed, and put on my dressing gown and slippers. Outside one of the worst sou'westers in years was in full sway. I could hear the rain lashing against the panes of my turret windows. It was too dark to see anything, but I could hear the constant crashing of waves against the rocks below.

I opened my door to find Father there, already dressed in his oilskins.

"I thought you might be up," he said. "Looks like we're going to have one of our nights of real fun."

"It doesn't sound very funny to me, Father!" I said. "I think it's going to be a bad one."

Elsie appeared with her hair in rollers, carrying a storm lantern. I smiled.

"What are you doing with that, Elsie?" I teased her. "Waiting for the ship to sink?"

She tossed her head.

"Don't 'ee mock me, Miss Samantha. You may need this light when yourn go out!"

And at that moment there came a crack of thunder, and the electric lights did indeed go out. The Folly was plunged in darkness. I heard Elsie's cackling laugh as I borrowed the lantern to find some warm clothing and oilskins, which I hurriedly pulled on. Then we all three made our way downstairs.

"I daresay the old trouble's afoot," growled my father. "Water pouring into the utility room and messing up our generator. The electricity chaps warned me that it wouldn't stand another soaking. Sam, phone old Wimble and ask him to come up here. He'll get the generator going if anyone can."

I phoned old Wimble. He had been Father's electrician and plumber for the past forty years. Old as he now was, he didn't mind being awakened, and he said he'd come if Father asked him to, storm or not.

"Take care you don't get blown over the cliff, Wimble," I warned him, knowing how strong the wind would be gusting across the headland.

Meanwhile, we took out every lantern and oil lamp we could find. A second and then a third wave crashed over the terrace and poured into the utility room, demolishing the outside door as if it were matchwood. The water seeped under the inner door into the house, and soon we were ankle deep in it. It was bitterly cold. The noise was infernal. Wave after wave smashed against the stone balustrade of the terrace.

Within the next half hour old Wimble arrived with his two sons. They bailed out the utility room and nailed supports across the shattered door to keep it in place. Elsie and I were kept busy picking bits of seaweed, driftwood, and cork from the ground floor of the Folly, all the flotsam that would be littering the sands of the bay tomorrow.

I was almost happy. There was no time to think of Greg; no time for suspicions or emotions. I was up against a concrete enemy — the sea.

When at last the wind died down and

the storm abated, I was totally exhausted, wet and shaking. But I felt happy as Father poured rum for his 'crew' and Elsie and I shared a pot of strong tea. There would be plenty of work tomorrow mopping up, but meanwhile we could congratulate ourselves on having kept the raging ocean at bay.

8

By the following morning my resolve to withhold my love from Greg until he told me why he was excluding me from his life was beginning to weaken. Not that I changed my mind about the principle. I simply could not bear any kind of rift between us. I loved him.

I would almost certainly have eaten my pride and telephoned him that evening, but during the afternoon Father had an unexpected visitor. We were sitting in front of the log fire in the library when the door knocker roused William from his slumbers into a storm of furious barking. Elsie came in a moment later to announce that a Commander McMiller wished to speak to Father privately.

"McMiller? Don't know anyone of that name!" Father said, but he put down his pipe and went out to the hall to see his caller. He took him into the drawing room where they remained a good hour. Father did not bring the commander to the library for a drink or to meet me but showed him out of the house himself.

When at last he rejoined me, he looked tired and dejected. Whoever his visitor had been, he had not exactly cheered Father into a jovial mood.

"Think I'll have a whisky!" Father said. "How about you, Sammy. Sherry? Dubonnet?"

I shook my head. I had not wanted a drink since I came out of the hospital.

"Not bad news, Father?" I asked. I was worried. He looked suddenly so old.

He splashed some soda into his glass, and I was surprised to see him take a long drink before he came to sit down opposite me near the fireplace.

"Very bad news, I'm afraid!" He paused as if unsure how to continue. Then he said: "McMiller thought I should keep it from you for the present, but I'm not sure that would be right, under the circumstances."

My hand went to my mouth. It was dry, and I felt confused and afraid.

"Is it about Greg?"

I knew the answer even before Father nodded.

"It's all a bit of a mystery at the moment."

Fear made me angry.

"I'm sick and tired of all these mysteries!" I cried. "Greg won't tell me anything, and now here you are talking in riddles. Whatever it is, *I want to know*, Father."

144

With infuriating deliberation he relit his pipe. It was not his intent to keep me in suspense. I knew that. But he seemed to find it difficult to speak. Father, who was never at a loss for words! I was really frightened now.

"Father, please!" I begged.

"Yes, darling. Well, Commander McMiller is from Naval Intelligence. He came to see me because I've known Greg all his life and I suppose I am a fairly reliable person to give an opinion of the boy, being ex-navy and all that. I know this will be as great a shock to you as to me, but apparently McMiller seems to have some doubts about Greg. He is doing a check on him."

"On Greg!"

But even as I gasped out my disbelief, I was not really surprised. I, myself, had been trying to check up on Greg. So had Jolly . . .

"Go on," I said quickly as I saw him glance anxiously at my face.

"Greg's superiors are concerned because he's been spending so much money," he said. "They think he may be getting into debt. McMiller was trying to find out where Greg is getting the money."

"Isn't that Greg's business?" I was suddenly resentful that Greg's privacy should be subject to investigation. Why should the navy care? I said as much to Father.

"It depends very much on what is at the back of Greg's new-found affluence," Father said gravely. I know my face must have been flushed and my eyes flashing because he added: "You've got to listen calmly, Samantha, and not fly off the handle. It's much too serious for you to go off the deep end. This is a time to keep your cool, as Jolly would say."

I took a deep breath. Father was right. But I was not finding it easy to keep cool.

"So where does Commander McMiller think Greg's money is coming from?"

Father took another drink. He would not meet my eyes as he replied quietly:

"From a woman Greg meets regularly in a hotel bar in Trenoun!"

I caught my breath. It was almost a relief to have my fears confirmed.

"I see. From the redhead Jolly saw him with. Father, *you* don't believe that, do you? Greg taking blackmail money from a woman?"

"No one mentioned blackmail, Sammy!"

"Then why else would she give him money? Not even you, Father, can suspect Greg of being a gigolo!"

Father's face softened into a half smile.

"No!" he agreed. But his eyes became serious very quickly as he added. "But Greg's superiors seem to think he may be rather deeply involved — and she's a married woman."

He finished his whisky and stood up to pour himself another. I was almost as much scared by Father's unusually rapid drinking as by the things he had said.

He turned back to me.

"I told McMiller I trust Greg implicitly and don't think him capable of anything underhand. He has the highest morals, and I believe in his integrity. I've known him all his life, and I'm sure there's a perfectly reasonable explanation for everything. I suggested the best thing he could do was to question Greg at once and let him answer for himself."

I stayed silent. If McMiller were to meet the same stone wall I had met when I questioned Greg, he wouldn't be much the wiser.

Father finished his drink.

"I'm afraid, though, they tried this, and Greg refused to give an account of himself. You must appreciate, Sam, that Greg and Jolly's training is very hush-hush. Highly secret. This means that any of them could be a potential security risk if he were open to blackmail. It's my opinion, although McMiller never actually came out with it, that this is why they are concerned about Greg.

"That's ridiculous!"

"I agree and told McMiller so. However, I do understand his need to be certain. He went to see Tibby before he came to me. You'd better telephone her, darling. She must be terribly worried and shocked. I thought — I wondered if she would like the two of us to call 'round, let her know we, too, are supporting Greg."

"Oh, Father!" I ran to him and hugged him. It was so typical of him to be concerned for other people at a time like this. I hadn't given poor Aunt Tibby a thought. This must surely be a far greater shock to her than to me. I imagined the commander had not received much cooperation from her, either. Aunt Tibby would have tightened her mouth and flatly refused even to discuss Greg, with someone she would call 'an outsider'. I had my doubts as to whether she would say much even to me. As for Father . . .

Nevertheless, I did telephone her and give her Father's message. Aunt Tibby thanked me, politely enough, and asked me to thank Father but, as I had suspected, said she didn't see that there was any need for discussion. Surely we both knew that Greg could not possibly be involved in anything scandalous or unsavory. As far as she was concerned, that was the end of the matter. She was surprised I even listened to such nonsense, she added.

Father looked worried when I repeated this to him.

"I'm afraid it isn't going to be quite as simple as that!" he said, frightening me anew. "Not unless Greg can give a reasonable account of himself. I know these chaps; once they think they are on to something, they won't let go until they have all the facts. Jolly warned me last time he was here that something like this might happen if Greg didn't give a better account of his actions."

"Jolly warned *you*!" I echoed stupidly, surprised. He had also tried to warn me. My heart sank. Suddenly I found myself wishing that Greg had been having a straightforward love affair with the redhead. That would be something I could come to grips with. But now this ugly question of money!

Then all at once my fear subsided. Aunt Tibby was right. It was just not possible that Greg would be involved in anything unsavory. Greg, whom I loved better than anyone in the world, was so essentially good that it was hard to find any real flaw in his character. Father believed in him. Aunt Tibby believed in him. So must I. This was a mad nightmare from which we would all shortly awake.

"Trust me, darling. No matter what anyone says, trust me!" How many times he had repeated those words! Now, perhaps, the real significance of that request was becoming clear. *Greg had known this was going to happen.* That was why he had warned me.

I didn't voice these thoughts to Father. It was essentially a private matter between Greg and me. I even felt relieved that McMiller had brought it out into the open. Greg would at last be forced to explain everything to me, if to no one else. If there was some further need for secrecy, I would renew my promise to keep faith with him, whatever the navy and the world might say.

Father looked suddenly less disturbed. I think he was relieved because I seemed to be taking the whole affair more calmly. By unspoken mutual agreement we did not discuss it any further that evening.

I was disappointed but not altogether surprised that Greg did not telephone that evening and I did not phone him. It would have been difficult for me to talk normally without referring to the commander's visit, and Greg might not yet know about it. I

150

felt this was something we must discuss in person, face to face.

I went to bed early and slept well. In the morning I woke with the same feeling of relief. I was quite convinced that it was only a matter of time before Greg told me all I'd need to know to confirm his complete innocence. Then we would be able to begin our marriage again, this time with no secrets between us.

Two days later Greg came home on weekend leave. He looked thin and dejected, but there was a defiance in the flash of his eyes that gave him a strange look of pride. His voice, too, was defiant as he walked into the library at the Folly, surprising both Father and me, and apologized for not letting us know beforehand that he was arriving.

Father cleared his throat, obviously embarrassed and not quite sure of himself. I felt unaccountably shy. Greg and I had not seen each other since the night of our quarrel, and I wasn't sure whether he would come and kiss me or would wait for me to make the first move.

"Would you like some tea?" I asked in a silly, formal little voice.

"Thanks. That would be nice!" he replied, equally formal.

I escaped to the kitchen where Elsie was

making pastry. When she heard that 'Master Greg' was home, her wrinkled old face lit up with pleasure. She adored Greg and had always spoiled him even more than she had spoiled Jolly and me.

"Do 'ee make the tea, Miss Samantha, whilst I go light the fires in the guest wing," she said. "It's a bitter wind."

I had not yet considered whether Greg and I would return to our own private wing together. But Elsie's assumption that we would be using the rooms solved the problem for me. I had no wish to remain alone in my solitary turret!

I took the tea tray into the library and was somewhat taken aback to hear Father and Greg having a heated discussion about the Arab-Israeli war. I poured out the tea and covertly watched Greg's face. He looked animated and interested and years younger. Something Father said made him laugh — a young, amused laugh. This was Greg — the boy I'd always known and loved — back with us as he'd been before our marriage. Tremendous love for him welled up in me. I longed to be alone with him upstairs.

"Elsie is lighting the fires in the guest wing," I told him, suddenly shy again. "When you've had tea, I expect you'd like to go up and change."

"Oh, thanks!" Greg replied, avoiding my eyes. "I'll fetch my bag."

I wondered if he had been so unsure of his welcome that he'd left his clothes in the car ready to drive down to Trevellyan Hall if Father or I had objected to his presence at the Folly. Usually he brought his bags in with him.

He did not come back into the library but went upstairs, leaving me with Father. I plucked up courage and took the initiative. One of us had to break the ice!

So I followed Greg upstairs, William scampering after me, barking excitedly from the pleasure of having Greg home again. However, I did not let him into our rooms. I opened the door and went inside to Greg, alone.

9

Greg was unpacking. I sat down on the bed, hands folded in my lap, hoping he would speak, but he ignored me. After a few minutes the silence became unbearable, so I said:

"Lovely to have you home, darling!"

Greg swung round and gave me a dark look. I felt the colour rush to my cheeks.

"Not exactly in the most agreeable circumstances!" he said, turning back to his unpacking. His voice sounded harsh, almost sarcastic. "You realize, I suppose, that I'm under a cloud?"

I sensed the pain behind these abrupt words.

"Yes, I know. Did Father tell you we'd had a visit from Commander McMiller?"

Again Greg swung around to look at me. This time his eyes were narrowed, and he looked almost desperate.

"Yes! Suppose you tell me about it!"

As briefly as I could, I recounted the little I knew. Greg's face registered no surprise. As my voice faltered into silence, he said:

"Yes, well, the idea of blackmail is a load

of nonsense. I hope neither you nor your father took it seriously. Of all the crazy ideas . . . "

I bit my lip. At long last Greg was about to talk to me.

"Please explain things to me, Greg," I urged him on.

"I'll try!" His voice was flat, emotionless. "As far as blackmail is concerned, forget it. I ask you, would I have gone openly to a local pub and extorted money from my victim! It's about the craziest idea anyone could entertain."

I nodded. I thought so, too.

"That's what Father and I said," I told him. "But Greg, what exactly *were* you doing? And what are the authorities making inquiries about? *Why* are you under a cloud?"

Greg's face tightened.

"I thought you already knew most of the answers," he said. "I've been meeting a married woman friend. The unofficial navy inquiries are to check up on my explanation and to make sure the facts tally."

"What explanation? What facts?"

"So you still don't know!" Greg's harsh tone of voice shook me.

"Greg, whatever it is, I'll stand by you. Why is it so hard for you to tell me what this is all about?"

"I didn't want to have to," Greg sounded weary now. His face looked old and immensely sad. "I didn't want to be the one to have to hurt you, Sam. I suppose I've been a coward, but I hoped someone else would discredit me in your eyes. That it wouldn't have to come from me."

I felt my heart hammering.

"Greg, I want to know — from *you*! Not from anyone else."

He paused for just a moment, then he said softly: "Okay, so I have a mistress. Her name is Jane Swan. She's thirty-three. She lives in London. She's half Hungarian and very, very rich. She's in love with me, and because she is, she insists on giving me things — expensive things. The car. The case of champagne I sent you. A gold cigarette lighter. And cash. Lots and lots of lovely cash!"

I simply did not believe him. Had I done so, I think I might have jumped off the bed and hit him. But I thought he was joking. I told him it was no time to invent stupid stories. I wanted the truth. He looked at me bitterly then.

"Well, you're going to have to accept it sooner or later, Sam. You see, it is the truth — the whole unpalatable truth. I suppose it's useless saying I'm sorry. At least I can

156

tell you I have never loved her; never loved anyone but you. But I don't think that will matter much, will it? Jane Swan was my mistress. She's rich, and she loves me, so she gave me money. It's as simple as that."

I was silenced. Greg could not be saying these things as a joke. It would be too cruel. Yet I still could not believe they were true.

"In one breath you say you love me, and in another you say you have a mistress who gives you . . . " Then my voice broke. Greg took a step toward me but stopped, then turned away. It was as if he could not bear the horror and dawning credulity on my face.

"I knew you wouldn't understand, Sam. I didn't expect you to, any more than I expect you to forgive me. The affair is over now, of course. I shan't be seeing her again."

I felt icy cold.

"You mean because the authorities have stepped in and put a stop to it? Not because you wished it yourself."

"Exactly! It seems my behaviour is considered unbecoming to an officer and a gentleman. I shall certainly not be promoted, and quite possibly I will be chucked out of the course and sent somewhere else. That is, if they don't throw me out of the navy altogether."

For a moment my horror and self-pity were swamped by pity for Greg. The navy was his life. This disgrace would finish him. But my pity did not last long. A hot, fierce anger exploded in me.

"You lied to me!" I accused him. "You gave me your word that she didn't mean anything to you and that you hadn't been unfaithful. You told me to trust you. *Trust you!*" My voice rose higher. "And I so nearly did!"

Greg lit a cigarette. The only emotion he showed was in the trembling of his hands.

"I'm sorry I have hurt you!" he said under his breath.

I was not just hurt. My whole life had crashed into ruins, and Greg spoke as though he'd merely broken a favourite toy.

"And what about our marriage, Greg?"

"That's up to you. I expect you'll want a divorce. I don't expect you to see me through this. After all, why should you?"

With one of those abrupt changes of mood, I now felt calm.

"Do *you* want a divorce, Greg?"

I heard his quick indrawn breath.

"Naturally not! I love you. I know you won't be able to believe that, but it's true."

I was aware it was utter madness to believe him. Logic told me not even to consider

158

it. Yet my heart betrayed me. Besides, somewhere deep inside me I felt that he really did love me. Perhaps his kind of loving was not like mine. Infidelity was one thing, but the lies, the deception ... his actually accepting gifts from that woman, money ...

I felt sick. I wanted to hate him, yet could not. He was mine. He had to be. Never hers.

"But Greg, *why?*" I asked helplessly. "You weren't all that hard up, were you? We could have managed on your pay. I was going back to work. I didn't really want those flowers. We didn't need the car. I don't understand."

"Try not to think about it," he interrupted. "I'm just weak; that's all I can say. Jane offered me these things, insisted I take them, and I was tempted and took them. I'll get rid of them now, of course."

I was shocked by the casual way he spoke about such things. It was as if he were talking about a basket of apples, as if he had no sense of morality, no idea of the seriousness of what he had done. And no real understanding of what he had done to me.

"What about your career? What if they do — fling you out?"

Greg shrugged.

"I suppose I'd just have to find myself a job."

"But the navy's your life!" I suddenly remembered. "Greg, who was Mr. Richards?"

I noted the quick flicker of his eyelids. Intuition told me he was about to tell me a lie. Another, I thought bitterly. But his voice sounded matter-of-fact enough as he replied:

"No one important. Just a divorce detective. Someone Jane's husband put on to her."

I had no reason to doubt that, so I let it drop.

Downstairs, Elsie rang the dinner gong. I had no idea how much time had elapsed while we had talked. Hurriedly I brushed my hair and put on a clean blouse.

"We'd better go down and eat," I said, although I certainly had no appetite and doubted if Greg had, either.

As I toyed with my food, I thought: Nothing has been resolved. Greg and I were not only unreconciled, but the gulf between us had widened so much — despite the solution to all the mysteries — that I could not see how it could be closed. Jane Swan. *Jane Swan!* Her name buzzed around my brain like a bedtime mosquito, giving me no peace. Beautiful. Hungarian. Rich. Greg's mistress! He had lain with her, made love to her. She loved him. Loved him enough to try to buy his affection with her riches. Greg was a gigolo. Or almost. Greg, who said he loved me, at the same time loving her body . . .

"For the third time, Samantha, will you have some more wine?"

Father's voice brought me out of the clouds. I realized I was in the dining room. We were at dinner. Father knew nothing yet. If he *knew*, would he allow Greg to sit there at the table, half hidden by the green candles? A husband who had betrayed me. How *could* Greg sit there toying with his food, keeping up a conversation with Father about shooting and dogs and twelve bore guns as though he had never put our marriage and our love in jeopardy? Did he really have no idea how he had publicly humiliated me? Commander McMiller, Jolly, his fellow officers, probably all his superiors, must know he had had a rich mistress and therefore that, I, his wife of only a few months, was totally inadequate.

My cheeks burned. I trembled as I looked across the table. Greg was talking to Father, and his face was in profile — high, straight forehead, nicely shaped brow above wide, honest eyes. *Honest!* Such a word was a parody of the truth! Then I found myself questioning my criticism. It could be argued that honest, guileless Greg had been so incapable of an underhand affair that he had carried on *his* affair practically in public. It could be that his very openness had landed him now in a disastrous mess. Honest but foolish. Yet Greg was not a fool.

Then again, who was I, an inexperienced girl, to judge whether a mistress of Jane Swan's undoubted fascinations could not make a fool of a clever young man if she so chose? One would have supposed her to be a fool, too, since it must have been obvious her affair with Greg would be found out sooner or later, so blatantly had they behaved.

My mind revolved in endless circles. I wanted to find excuses for Greg, but I could not. Whether or not Jane Swan had been Greg's mistress before he married me, he should not have continued with the association after. There was no excuse for that. Could sex have such a hold on a man that he could not give up a woman even if he wanted to?

I was reminded of my own desperate need of Greg. That had not been so easily put aside the night in the hotel at Trenoun when I'd wanted him to make love to me even though I knew there were barriers between us; even though I suspected he had another woman in his life. I had had no pride, no real will to subdue my longing for him.

But I loved him! And Greg had sworn he did not and never had loved Jane Swan. Was it love that had weakened me? Or sex? Was it love that had driven her to pursue him so ruthlessly?

I pushed aside my plate, knowing I could not finish the meal Elsie had lovingly prepared — soup, roast duck, apple pie. I could not eat. I gulped down some more wine and felt my head swimming. I tried to imagine what life would be like without Greg. I had never been without him. If I did divorce him, he could not go on living at Trevellyan Hall, nor I at the Folly. To have to see him and yet not to speak to him . . . It was a frightful, impossible prospect!

"If you aren't going to finish the pie, we'll go to the library and have coffee." Father brought me back to reality again.

"I have a bit of a headache," I told him. "I think I'll go straight up to bed if you and Greg will excuse me."

I knew I couldn't face an evening chatting as though nothing were wrong, nothing had happened. Greg might be able to do so but I could not.

I retired, of course, to my own turret bedroom. Elsie came in with a hot-water bottle and looked at me shrewdly.

"Did 'ee have a lover's tiff?" she asked. "Don't 'ee let the sun set on your anger, Miss Samantha. It don't do!"

"I'm not feeling well." I hoped she would believe me. "It's better for Greg and me to be in different rooms when I'm not well."

I don't think I convinced her, but she went out, leaving me alone. I flung myself on my bed and covered my eyes with both hands. I think the tension of the past hours, if not days, must have taken a bigger toll than I realized, for surprisingly I fell asleep. I woke to hear footsteps on the turret stairs. My heart jolted. Was this Greg coming to find me? To talk to me? Did I want him to?

I both did and did not. But I had no choice in the matter. It was Father. He knocked and came in, apologizing for disturbing me. He looked an old, broken man.

"You've been talking to Greg!" I said. "He's told you what has been happening?"

Father nodded and sat down in the same chair beside my bed he used to sit in when I was a little girl, when he read me bedtime stories or told me exciting tales of the Cornish sea. Impulsively I held out my hand, and he took it and held it tight. It was as if he had come to me for comfort rather than to offer it to me.

"Greg's gone back to the Hall," he told

164

me. "I felt it would be best; in fact, I insisted. I cannot have him here under my roof." His voice became husky with emotion. "Samantha, I never thought I'd have to close my door to Greg; your husband, too! But old-fashioned though you may think me, I cannot condone his behaviour. He, himself, offers no excuse, and I can find none." He looked at me searchingly. "I suppose you still love him, in spite of everything?"

"I suppose so!"

Father nodded as if expecting this reply.

"The trouble with people like us, my darling, is that we don't love easily, and when we do, it's for all time. I knew in my heart you'd feel that way about Greg despite the way he has treated you. His behaviour has been quite disgraceful, despicable. I still find it hard to believe."

"Did he tell you everything?"

"I imagine so. I don't want to think about the sordid details. Goodness only knows what his brother officers are thinking, saying."

"Greg said the navy might throw him out. Surely, Father, adultery — " My voice quivered on the word " — is a civil, not a naval offence?"

"Any scandal that affects one of its officers is a matter of concern to the navy. However, I doubt he'd be court-martialled for such an offence. He will most probably be severely reprimanded and told to behave himself in the future. He may well find himself posted elsewhere. I have no need to tell you that whatever my personal feelings about the way he has treated you, I'll do what I can for him. My name still carries some weight in the navy."

"That's really good of you, Daddy!" I used the old childish name. There were tears in my eyes. I knew very well how shocked he must be. No matter what suspicions we'd either of us held until now, neither of us had really believed Greg could behave in such a squalid way. We'd both supposed that when he chose to do so, he would adequately explain away his strange behaviour.

Father patted my hand.

"I think it might help if you, too, wrote to his commanding officer. Say you're standing by your husband because you know this was only a temporary lapse, that your miscarriage might have put too great a strain on him. Make them feel sympathetic towards the boy." He gave me a searching look. "You *are* going to stand by him, Samantha?" he asked anxiously.

I had not been sure until then, but at that moment I was sure. I'd do anything I could to help Greg reinstate himself in the navy.

But that did not mean I was prepared to be a real wife to him in private.

"I'll go down to the Hall and talk to him tomorrow," I told Father. "If he agrees, I'll move into the stable flat with him. That way, we won't be a nuisance either to you or Aunt Tibby. This is our worry, not yours."

"Nonsense! It reflects on the whole family — on both families," Father said gruffly. "We've got to give the boy moral support. But I won't have him back under my roof. At least not until I feel he has redeemed himself. You understand, my dear?"

I understood. Just as I understood that as far as the outside world was concerned, I had to show that I still believed in Greg and thought well enough of him to wish to remain his wife. That was why I must go and live with him.

I did not realize quite how hard that task would be.

10

I felt depleted and nervous as I walked
William across the dunes toward the Hall
the following morning. The air was soft and
mild. There was real warmth in the sunshine
that glinted on the golden sands and sparkled
on the sea. The tide was out, and the rippled
sandy beach was as clean and fresh as the
soft green blades of grass beginning to shoot
up on either side of the little lane leading to
Greg's home.

I was familiar with every foot of this walk
between our two houses. I had so often
picked violets along these hedgerows, looked
for birds' nests, smelled wild dog roses
and brambles, picked blackberries for Aunt
Tibby's autumn jelly. I'd seen the stunted
hawthorn tree bent farther and farther upon
its side by the gale-force winds until now it
was almost horizontal but nonetheless always
a glory of white blossom in the spring.

It seemed to me that this was perhaps the
first real day of summer. Yet I felt none
of the usual elation and welling of life
within me. On any other day I would have
been singing suitable songs like 'First Came

the Primrose', and 'Now the North Wind Ceases, The Warm South-west Awakes,' and my favourite: 'A White Rose.' But today I could not bring myself to voice those words:

The red rose whispers of passion,
And the white rose breathes of love;
O, the red rose is a falcon
And the white rose is a dove

But I send you a cream-white rosebud
With a flush on its petal tips;
For the love that is pure and sweetest
Has a kiss of desire on the lips.

The red roses that Greg had sent me with his love had been paid for by another woman. I would never sing that song again.

"Excuse me!"

My eyes were so blinded by tears, I had not seen the man approaching across the dunes. He came hurrying toward me, raising a rather ridiculous little black homburg and revealing a pointed bald pate. He had a thin, white, weasel-type face and a short thin body in a neatly pressed black suit. He wore a little bow tie.

"Excuse me, miss, but could you tell me the way to Trevellyan Hall?"

I was instantly attentive and, because I had taken such a quick, unfair dislike to him, tried my hardest to be ultra polite.

"I'm on my way there myself. Perhaps I could show you?"

A faint smile flitted across his face. He fell into step beside me. Every now and again I felt rather than saw him staring at me.

"I just came off the bus from Newquay," he said. "Someone misdirected me. I'm quite lost."

"Oh, we're only a few hundred yards from the Hall," I told him. "It isn't easy to see the gateway from the lane. I expect you walked right past it."

"Probably I did!" He gave me yet another covert look. "You aren't by any chance from Trevellyan Hall?"

I couldn't place his accent. It seemed to me to be a London one, but there was a hint of some other dialect in it.

"No, I live at Tristan's Folly. Over there!" I pointed to the headland behind us.

I saw his face register surprise, then quickly close up.

"You wouldn't, by any chance, be Mrs. Trevellyan?"

The name sounded quite unfamiliar, and I nearly denied it. The villagers had all continued to call me Miss Jolly since my marriage, and apart from booking into the hotel in Trenoun as Lieutenant and Mrs. Gregory Trevellyan, I don't think I'd ever used my new name.

If the stranger noticed my awkward "yes," he paid no obvious attention to it.

"Your husband is a friend of mine. I'm on my way to see him," he said calmly.

We turned into Trevellyan drive. As we did, I had a strange intuition.

"You're Mr. Richards, aren't you?"

It was a shot in the dark, but it clearly hit home. He could not hide his surprise.

"How did you know I was coming?" The question was asked in a quick, nervous voice.

"I didn't! I just guessed it was you." I had no wish to talk to him further. If this was an example of one of Greg's friends, I preferred to have as little as possible to do with him. I wondered how this nasty little man had known Greg would be at the Hall. Greg, himself, had not left the Folly until late the previous night and that on the spur of the moment.

However, for the time being I was more concerned with getting my companion into the Hall and off my hands as quickly as possible. I am not usually so positive about sudden likes and dislikes, but I felt a real antipathy toward Mr. Richards.

Greg did not seem particularly pleased to see him either, although he was obviously surprised and delighted to see me.

"Oh, it's you!" he said to Mr. Richards with none of his usual courtesy. He smiled at me and said:

"Aunt Tibby is in the kitchen, Sammy. The coffee's still hot!"

I took the hint and disappeared to the back of the house. Aunt Tibby, looking exactly as always (somehow I'd expected her to look different after all the emotional upheaval), was arranging flowers in a Lalique bowl.

"There's coffee on the hot plate," she said, as if nothing untoward had happened. It was like any other greeting any other morning.

"Those are pretty!" I said, admiring the colourful pansies. "There were one or two dog roses out as I came down the lane. I think summer has really come."

"About time, too," Aunt Tibby replied. She sighed. "I feel the winter more each year. This house is damp. I was telling Greg so last night. Gets into my bones."

I smiled. Aunt Tib enjoyed making herself out to be years older than she was.

"Gets into mine, too!" I teased.

A tiny smile played at her mouth but was

gone again as she said:

"Greg's got some leave, I hear. He came home last night."

So there was no mention of the fact that Father had banished Greg from Tristan's Folly.

"I know. As it is for a whole week, I thought maybe Greg and I could move into the flat," I said. "That is, if its ready."

"Ready enough!" Aunt Tibby sounded pleased. Perhaps Greg had told her the whole story. I hoped she'd find a way to discuss it with me. It was going to be difficult having conversations in which the most relevant facts were missing. "Have you brought any luggage?"

I shook my head.

"I thought I'd go back home for lunch and pack a few things and bring them down this afternoon. By the way, Greg has a visitor. A Mr. Richards!"

I watched her face as I mentioned the man's name. Aunt Tibby gave no sign of recognition, but I felt sure she had not forgotten those two strange telephone calls any more than I had.

"The man who phoned Greg," I prompted.

"Oh, yes." I knew it was no good trying to get anything more out of her.

At that moment Greg came in minus his

visitor, who was on his way back to the bus stop, he told us.

Aunt Tibby put a cup of coffee on the kitchen table near the one she had given me and left the room, ostensibly to put the pansies in an appropriate place. I said:

"I thought we might as well make use of the flat during your leave, Greg. Aunt Tib says it's fit to live in. If you agree, I'll bring my suitcase with a few clothes and other things this afternoon."

I surprised myself by my composure. But it did not last. As I looked at Greg's face I was horrified to see tears in his eyes. Greg crying! I could not believe it. I wanted to jump up, put my arms around him, and pull his head down to my breast. But I could not move. The memory of Jane Swan kept me virtually paralyzed.

"It seems a waste of Pentyre's work if we don't make use of the flat . . . " I went on talking meaninglessly, giving Greg time to recover. "And anyway, it's probably time we had a place of our own. Aunt Tibby approves of the idea, and so does Father." My voice faltered as I remembered what my father's name must mean to Greg now. "Anyway, if you agree . . . "

"Thank you, Sammy!"

Greg seemed more himself again. No, not

174

himself. But he had got the better of the tears that had threatened a moment ago. Otherwise, he remained cool and rather too polite, keeping me at arm's length. I suppose I was the same. It was not possible for either of us to be natural, not unless one or other of us started talking about the things that really mattered, the only thing that mattered: *us*.

I went back to the Folly for lunch and told Father and Elsie I'd be living with Greg at the flat until his leave ended. Father received this news without comment. Before I left my home, I sat down at my desk and wrote the letter Father had advised me to send to Greg's commanding officer. I gave it to Father to read before I sealed it.

"It won't do any harm, and it might do a lot of good!" was all Father said as he handed it back to me. "Shouldn't say anything to Greg about it if I were you."

I gave it to Elsie to post when she went into the village that afternoon. It was nearing tea time when I finally returned to Trevellyan. Greg, Aunt Tibby informed me, had gone out.

"He went into Newquay to sell his car," she said. "He'll be back by the four o'clock bus, I dare say."

My mouth felt dry. I never wanted to see that car again, and I prayed Greg would be successful in selling it. I wondered if this was the first step he was taking to reinstate himself. With the navy? Or with me? I wasn't sure.

When he returned, he made no mention of the sale, but he had walked from the village, so it was clear he had got rid of the car. We went to the flat. During the afternoon Aunt Tibby had been preparing for us. She had a fire going in the tiny living room fireplace. The big bed in the bedroom had clean sheets and blankets. The place looked warm and welcoming, and in other circumstances I would have felt happy and excited to be there. The Persian rug was not by the fireplace. Had Greg sold this in Newquay, too? I wondered. But I dared not ask him. However, I decided to make the first move to break the ice. I took off the silver-link bracelet Greg had given me and put it on the coffee table.

"You decide what to do with this!" I said. I spoke without any anger or bitterness. I might have been discussing an unwanted ashtray.

Greg's mouth tightened so obviously I knew at once that he was angry. Really angry.

"I bought that with my own money. With *my money*!" he almost shouted.

We both stared at the little silver pool of links.

"I told you. *I told you it was from me!*" His face was flushed, his eyes flashing.

I was suddenly angry, too.

"How was I supposed to know that? The roses were supposed to come from you, bought with *your* money. So was the champagne!"

His anger evaporated. So did mine as I saw his face take on the sad look of resignation with which I was beginning to become familiar.

"I'm sorry!" I said. "I thought — I didn't realize . . ."

"I know. I'm sorry, too. It's difficult for you, I'm afraid. For both of us."

With an effort I picked up the bracelet and fastened it on my wrist again. Greg made no comment. I wished I could think up some excuse to leave the room, but Aunt Tibby was cooking supper for us at the Hall, and I had no reason to escape to the kitchen. Nor did I wish to go into the bedroom where I could have occupied my nervous hands unpacking the few things I had brought from home.

Greg seemed unable to do anything but walk up and down, obviously ill at ease. William bounded in and saved the situation for both of us. He gave us a topic of safe conversation and a reason not to look at one another. Somehow we remained at arm's length in the tiny apartment until Aunt Tibby came across the courtyard to tell us supper was ready.

We both lingered on at the Hall to watch television that night, Greg no more interested in the programme than I was but about as reluctant as I to return to the little bedroom where we would once more be flung into close proximity. The situation was of my making, and I felt that it was up to me to try to make it easier for both of us, so I suggested as casually as I could that it was high time we went to bed. Greg said he would take William for a last run. I was grateful that he was giving me the chance to undress and have my bath in privacy. When he returned, I was already in bed.

"It's raining!" he said, standing in the bedroom door looking at me with strange remote eyes. "A soft, fine drizzle. If it's like this tomorrow, I thought we might go fishing."

Momentarily I forgot all that lay between us. I sat up in bed hugging my knees. One of the pastimes I most enjoyed was fishing with the boys. Sometimes we went inland to the river; other times we went for mackerel in the sea, trailing lines behind the dingy and hauling the fish on board as fast as we could hook them.

"Yes, that would be great fun," I began enthusiastically. "I haven't done any fishing since . . . " I broke off, remembering with pain the time before our wedding. Would those happy, carefree, beautiful days ever come back? Could Greg and I ever return to the former simple companionship of our childhood? Somehow I could not believe it.

When Greg finally slipped into bed beside me, I pretended to be asleep. It was far from easy, so terribly aware of him was I. I could hear his uneven breathing and feel him moving restlessly beside me. Though I tried not to, I could not stop thinking of other nights we had shared when the mere idea of sleep would have seemed laughable, so intense was our bodies' need for contact. And Greg had been the more passionate, the more urgent of the two, I catching fire from him and finally matching his desire with my own.

The inevitable thought of Jane Swan made me give a little gasp of pain. Greg must have heard it because instantly he said:

"Are you all right, Sammy? I thought you were asleep."

"No!" It was the only word I could force

from between my clenched lips.

"I expect it's the strange bed," Greg said without any real conviction in his voice. "It'll take time to get used to it."

I found my voice. In the darkness I said:

"I expect it will take us time to get used to lots of things."

I spoke with bitterness, and it was obviously clear to Greg. He said quietly:

"I understand how you feel!"

"Do you?" I was suddenly wide awake. "Can you really understand what it's like to imagine the husband you love, making love to another woman? Suppose I had been unfaithful to you, Greg? Just suppose!"

"Darling, don't, please!"

Even his endearment could not stop me, now I had begun to open my heart.

"Why not? Why shouldn't you suffer just a little? Why should I be the one to have all the pain?"

Even as I spoke I knew I was being unfair. Greg had been suffering, too. I would never forget those tears in his eyes and his changed face. I felt ashamed of my childishness, but I still could not forgive or forget.

"Would you like me to make you a cup of tea?"

His kindness angered me further.

"No, thanks!"

180

"Is there anything at all you want?"

"Yes!" I said quietly but with pent-up violence. "I want you to explain, Greg. I want you to make me understand. I *want* to understand."

"There isn't anything more I can say," Greg's quiet voice replied after a brief pause. "If I had any way of making all this easier for you, believe me I would. I can only say again that I love you. I love *you*. I have never loved anyone else."

"And why should I believe you?"

"No, I suppose that isn't easy. Nevertheless, it's true. I love you with all of my heart."

When I answered, my voice still held a stinging bitterness.

"You mean you *want* me, don't you? You're confusing sex with love."

Now it was Greg's turn to be really angry. He twisted around to face me and caught hold of my arm. The grip of his fingers was painful.

"It isn't I who am confused. It's you, Sam. I think you've stopped loving me, but *you* still want me, don't you? Well, I'm not denying I want you, too. No living man could lie here beside you and not want you, damn it. But don't say I don't love you because I do. Do you hear me, I do, *I do!*"

Suddenly we were in each other's arms, kissing with a fierce desperation that had no room for tenderness. It was the same violent passion that had engulfed us that night in the hotel. We fought, wrestled, clung to one another, hungry, frightened, excited, and unhappy. I know that beneath the tumult of my physical desire, I was mentally resisting Greg. To love him this way when I could not be sure I still respected him or loved him as a person was a self-inflicted humiliation that took its toll. I could find no relief. Greg knew it. His voice, husky and pleading, reached my consciousness.

"Don't fight me. Don't resist me. I love you. *I love you!*"

I finally feigned my response. As Greg's weight slackened across my body, and he rolled gently away from me, he was as aware as I of the failure of our love making. I felt hot tears running down my cheeks. Greg reached over and gently wiped them away with a corner of the sheet.

"I'm sorry, darling. So very sorry!" he whispered.

I could not bring myself to reply. I did not want him to apologize. I did not want him to be unhappy, abject, apologetic. I wanted everything to be the way it used to be, with none of these terrible things that had come between us. Childishly, I wanted to turn the clock back and for me to believe in Greg again. My hero had crashed from his pedestal, and I wanted him the way I'd always thought of him — as perfect.

For the second time that night, I turned away from him and pretended to be asleep.

11

At least Greg's disgrace had one good result. I was no longer heartbroken about my miscarriage. Now I understood why he had not been anxious to become a father, and I, for certain, had no wish to have a baby under the present circumstances. I made up my mind to return to my nursing training as soon as Matron could reinstate me. I wished to make myself independent of Greg. I hated the idea of having to ask him for money.

Jolly did not come home on leave. I understood why when he wrote a miserable letter to me.

I'm afraid Greg's name stands none too high in the wardroom. Everyone is speculating as to whether or not he'll be allowed to stay on the course and opinions seem fairly equally divided. I try to stick up for him, but it isn't easy. I simply cannot forgive him for doing this to you, and naturally I don't much like the backwash I have to put up with as Greg's friend.

. . . But it is the casual, callous way he

has so hurt you that makes me feel I'd really rather not see too much of him in future. Obviously, for your sake, I won't break with him completely, but I shall try not to coincide our leaves.

Do you know how Father is taking it? Pretty badly, I imagine, as it is the kind of thing he'd abhor and is so foreign to anything in his nature. Mind you, Sam, I still find it hard to believe Greg capable of behaving as he seems to have done. There must have been a weakness in his character we never suspected.

Are you all right, Sammy? I worry about you a lot and would welcome a letter from you.

I wrote at once, explaining that Father would not have Greg under his roof but that he was doing what he could to help Greg for my sake. He had even made the long train trip to London to see some influential contacts at the Admiralty. Aunt Tibby, as was to be expected, had refused to discuss the matter at all and to all intents and purposes was behaving as if nothing had happened. As for myself, I was toughening up, or perhaps growing up, at last. Like Father, I stood solidly by Greg, but I could not as yet find it in my heart to forgive him, although he was doing everything he could to make amends.

He was, indeed, doing all he could to make life tolerable. It cannot have been easy for him, with the verdict on his future hanging in the balance. I know he was under great strain from this, apart from the inevitable withdrawal of my love. Pride forbade me giving any demonstration of affection, and we lived together as two rather excessively polite and tolerant friends.

There were one or two days when we were nearly happy: the day when we went fishing and momentarily forgot our adult status as we splashed barefoot on the rocks, soaking the turned-up legs of our jeans and behaving as if we were kids again; the day when we walked William across the cliffs, racing one another over the springy turf now thick with pink sea daisies, venturing so far we had to take the bus home; the day when we went to the market and bought second-hand bargains for the flat, returning home triumphantly with a pretty hand-carved ashtray, a huge white Victorian water jug with violets painted on it for flowers, and an old-fashioned laundry basket we made into a new bed for the fast growing William.

But these times were rare, and for the most part we tended to avoid being alone together. Often we were at the Hall with Aunt Tibby, or when I found the atmosphere too awkward, I would walk home to spend the afternoon playing chess with Father or helping him to re-plant the wooden tubs on the terrace.

Greg's week's leave passed in this way, and suddenly it was time for him to go back to Trenoun. By now a decision must surely have been reached about his future, and I could see the acute tension in Greg as he began to pack his belongings. I forgot my resolve to be unemotional, and told him not to worry, that Father has said he was sure the navy would not court-martial him and that everything would sort itself out given time.

He looked at me from narrowed, anxious eyes.

"Does that go for you, too, Sammy? Are *you* going to be able to forgive me? Believe me or not, that's as important to me as being allowed to stay on the course."

"Don't . . . rush . . . me!" I brought the words out with difficulty. "I'm trying, Greg. I really am trying!"

He turned back to his suitcase, and his voice was controlled and level as he replied:

"Yes, I know. I'm grateful. You've made this week bearable. It could so easily have been otherwise!"

I felt a pang of guilt. Granted I had stood by Greg, had moved into the flat with him and reaffirmed publicly my position as his wife. But privately I had withheld any sign of affection, of love. Since that first night, I had turned my back on him, making it quite clear that I had no wish to make love. I could not really have made life very easy for him.

But I steeled my heart against such regrets. Greg had not exactly made my life easy for me before he had been found out and made to suffer for his behaviour. But for the navy's interference, he might still be enjoying his fortnightly visits to Jane Swan, I told myself. Moreover, he might still be taking money from her.

Sickened anew by thoughts I'd tried hard until now to put out of my mind, I was able to see Greg off on the bus next day without more than a casual wave of my hand and a brief "Good luck!"

"I'll telephone you!" Greg called back, his face suddenly distraught as if he could not bear this parting from me. For one moment I thought he was going to jump off the bus and run back to me, but I probably only imagined it. I turned, clutching William's lead and walked quickly away from the bus stop, unwilling for any passer-by to see my tears.

That afternoon I cleaned and tidied the flat, locked the door, and went back to the Folly. Father greeted me with his usual warmth. By tacit agreement Greg's name was not mentioned. The whole of the next day I busied myself helping old Elsie make a start on the spring cleaning. We were so engrossed in our work, therapeutic as far as I was concerned, that we did not hear the telephone ring. It was not until Father came upstairs to tell me Aunt Tibby had phoned with the news that Greg's future had been decided. He was not being posted away from the Trenoun.

I hugged Father with relief and excitement, begging him for further details which he was unable to give. Tibby, he said, had been understandably brief: she had so far never admitted that Greg's future was in doubt. However, Father, himself, was able to reveal a few facts he had not felt justified in passing on to me before the *fait accompli*. He had fought a long, hard battle at the Admiralty that day he'd gone to London; reminding the navy of the Trevellyans' gallant family history; talking of Greg's father; of Greg's own spotless record from school days through to Dartmouth; of his, Father's, belief in the boy and my faith in him. Before he left London, he had been promised that all these factors would be taken into account, and he had been given every reason to believe that Greg's misdemeanours would be overlooked this time.

My first instinct was to suggest to Father we celebrate this wonderful news. But the grimness of Father's face reminded me painfully that it wasn't really an occasion for congratulations. Greg had been helped out of a very unpleasant situation, and his reinstatement, if it could be so called, in no way lessened the unpleasantness of the whole wretched affair.

I did not, therefore, telephone Greg to say how happy I was for him. But I did write a rather stilted little note telling him I was very relieved for his sake, that I hoped he would not find it too hard picking up the threads again.

My letter crossed in the post with one from him.

You'll know by now from Aunt Tibby that I'm to be given another chance. I understand from my commanding officer that a great deal of the consideration afforded me was due to your father's intervention, as well as a letter from you. I am naturally very grateful to you both.

It is not very easy for me in the

wardroom; for obvious reasons I am none too popular, and I suppose one might truthfully say I am being put in Coventry. No doubt I have well deserved such punishment. I hope, in time, to get used to the isolation. I am more sorry for Jolly than for myself. I think he feels he should back me up but at the same time, his sympathies are with the other chaps, and of course, he would not want to be disloyal to you. Maybe you could drop him a line and tell him I neither expect nor wish him to show me any favours. So far as I am concerned, I feel I have forfeited any claim to his friendship.

My love as always,
Your Greg

I took the letter to my bedroom and read it several times. It was not difficult to read between the lines his feelings of humiliation, of bitterness at being ostracized, of hurt at the break with Jolly. There are people who are basically loners, who enjoy solitude and are self-sufficient. My husband was never like that. He was always gregarious, always popular, always immensely sociable. I knew that the detachment from his fellow officers would be a far greater anguish to Greg than to many others.

191

My self-imposed shell of indifference cracked with a painful pity. I wanted to dash off an impulsive letter telling him not to mind because I loved him, I was thinking of him, I still wanted him as my friend, believed in him. But I would not let myself do it. I felt I had gone along with him as far as I could. If Greg wanted more than this token of loyalty from me, he would have to earn it, and prove that he warranted my trust, my respect, my love. I knew that Father felt the same way. Perhaps Jolly did, too. None of us could reject Greg completely, but he had forfeited his right to be one of us. We closed ranks against him.

Only Aunt Tibby steadfastly refused to alter her feelings. She made it quite clear to me that in her eyes Greg was beyond guilt, beyond doubt, beyond criticism. Her complete faith in him irritated me. She was, I told myself, behaving like the proverbial ostrich, burying her head in the sand and firmly refusing to face facts. I wanted, on occasions, to shake her out of her complacency, force her to admit that Greg had openly confessed that he was guilty of every accusation levelled against him, that it was madness to go on trusting him in the face of this. Surely, I longed to shout at her, she knew that I would have given

Greg the benefit of the doubt if there was one, but there was not!

I was only able to voice these sentiments to Jolly, knowing that he felt exactly as I did. He had wanted as much as I to go on believing in his friend. My brother had loved Greg deeply and for as long as I had. We both felt betrayed.

"Do you think you can ever *really* feel the same about him again?" Jolly asked me as we walked over the wet sands during one of his short leaves. We had been talking around and around the same old painful subject. "I don't see how you can want to stay married to him after all this, Sam."

"I suppose because in some inexplicable way, I do still love him," I said truthfully. "I hate what he has done to me and to our marriage. I can't respect him anymore. I can't even trust him. But I can't imagine life without him. I just don't know about our future. I suppose time will sort it all out one way or another."

It was a relief to have Jolly to talk to. He described to me, even more vividly than Greg had done in his letter, how difficult life was for Greg in the wardroom and at work. Men, like children, could be cruel when they united against a colleague who had offended their society. No one spoke to Greg, unless necessary in the course of work. He was avoided at meal times, the chairs on either side of him being left conspicuously vacant.

"What does he do with himself when he's off duty?" I asked, my heart aching at the thought of his loneliness.

"Works, most of the time. He had two weeks backlog to catch up on, of course. But Greg wouldn't find that difficult. He's already way ahead of most of us. I've little doubt if he goes on as he is, he'll pass out of this course with all the honours. The fact is, Greg is brilliant. Probably that's one of the reasons the navy has let him stay at Trenoun."

Jolly gave a quick grimace.

"Getting top marks all the time doesn't exactly endear him to the others," he said, and I could hear in his voice his reluctant admiration of Greg's ability. "Poor old Greg! I have to admit it was decent of him to let me off the hook. I was feeling a bit of a Judas. I'm glad he understands."

I missed Jolly's companionship when his leave ended and realized that despite all the mental stress I had undergone, I was now physically fit again. It was time for me to go back to work and occupy my mind with something other than my unfortunate marriage and miscarriage.

I took the bus to Newquay and went to the hospital to see Matron. I was afraid that after so long an absence I might not be able to continue my training where I had left off, but she was hopeful about my prospects. Apparently I had been well thought of by my teachers. With plenty of extra study, Matron thought I stood every chance of regaining my place in the year's course.

Father approved of my decision. I know he took the view that any kind of activity that would keep me from brooding would be good for me. I would, of course, have to live in at the hospital, but I would be near enough in Newquay to get home to Tristan's Folly whenever I had time off.

I wrote and told Greg I would be resuming my training and that he should send letters to my old address in Newquay. In his reply he made no comment other than to ask me to let him know what date I would be leaving Tristan's Folly. I, therefore, had no idea how he felt about the possibility of my being away from home when he got leave. It was unlikely our free time would always coincide. Perhaps, like me, he had felt the strain of being alone together. Perhaps he welcomed the independent line I was taking. It did not concern me that Greg might resent my reaching this decision to go back to work without first consulting him. I took it for granted he had accepted the fact that he had forfeited the right to run my life.

The first few weeks back at the hospital I was so busy picking up the old threads that I had almost no time to think about myself or of Greg's problems. During the day I either attended lectures or assisted in the outpatient department. There was an acute shortage of staff because of an epidemic of influenza. At night, I studied until the early hours of the morning, then fell into bed too exhausted mentally and physically to want anything but sleep.

During my third week, however, I found that I was settling down well enough to feel stable again. I even became aware that the interest shown in me by the doctor with whom I worked in Outpatients, was not quite as impersonal as I had previously supposed. He had been particularly helpful and forebearing with me when I made inevitable mistakes.

Jimmy Planter was a good-looking young man of thirty, a first-class doctor with a fine reputation in the hospital. A quiet, sensitive, sympathetic approach drew his patients to him and inspired their confidence. Shortish, with crisp dark hair and bright brown eyes, he reminded me a little of Jolly. I liked him but did not really notice him as a person until the afternoon he asked me if I would go out for a drink with him when I came off duty.

"I'm sure you haven't left these hospital portals since you came here nearly a month ago," he said as I closed the door on the last patient — or what we both hoped was the last patient before we were relieved at the end of our session.

"I've had a great deal of work to catch up on," I told him. "Besides, I haven't really wanted to go out."

Jimmy Planter smiled at me with a grin so like Jolly's I had to remark on it. They obviously had the same attractive sense of humour and wonderful amiability.

"Damned if I want to remind you of your *brother*!" he said. "Now what about this drink? It would do you good, Samantha."

I smiled back at him, liking him very much. There was a warmth and friendliness in his eyes to which I found myself responding.

"Is that your prescription, Doctor?"

"For overwork and underplay, yes!"

It was easy enough with this lighthearted banter for me to say:

"You realize I am a respectable, married woman?"

I was surprised to see his face become suddenly serious.

"Yes, I know, damn it. Why is it all the nicest, prettiest girls already have husbands or boyfriends?"

"I'm sure there are dozens who haven't."

"Maybe, but they aren't the ones I fancy!" He toyed with a pencil, tapping it on the desk blotter "You know, Samantha, I noticed you the first time I ever saw you — a year or more ago, I suppose. You were a very young student nurse spending your first day in the ward — Children's Ward, wasn't it? You looked so incredibly young and innocent and dedicated — a young Florence Nightingale. After that, I often used to see you around the hospital. Then you disappeared with a dose of glandular fever, and I missed you."

I was flattered that he remembered so many details, but I didn't betray the fact.

"That's a good story!" I teased.

"But it's quite true. Someone — your friend Peggy, I think — told me you were getting married, and I thought I'd seen the last of you. Yet you turn up first as a patient and now as my assistant. It does call for a celebration."

I was tempted to have that drink with him. I think I might have weakened if I hadn't really liked him so much. But if there were a grain of truth in his story, it meant he found me attractive, and I wasn't interested in a flirtation, far less in the sort of affair that went on so often between nurses and doctors.

"I'm very much in love with my husband," I told him, feeling instantly embarrassed lest he should imagine I thought that his invitation inferred more than a friendly drink.

He nodded. Obviously he understood.

"I guessed as much. But thanks all the same for warning me. I'd still like to take you out for that drink. Your husband wouldn't object, would he? After all, it isn't a crime to have a drink with a married woman.

My heart jolted. Those same words had been used about Greg and Jane Swan.

Jane Swan! I felt a return of all the old hurt and bitterness. If Greg was so casual about his association with that woman he could hardly object to my spending an hour or two in Dr. Planter's company. There was no reason at all why I should refuse. I would very much enjoy a drink with him, and it could hurt no one.

"Okay! I'll meet you by the main gate. Half past six?"

Because by the time I was back in my quarters I was already regretting my impulsive acceptance, I dressed with particular care, defiantly going against my instinct that I was making a mistake. No matter what Greg might say or think, I was his wife. I felt guilty going out with another man.

But I went. And I enjoyed myself immensely.

Jimmy was far too sensitive and intelligent to force the pace. We had a quiet, companionable evening during which I learned with some surprise that he had already been married and was a widower. This had happened before he was twenty-three, and since that time he had remained a confirmed bachelor. As a medical student, he had fallen in love with a seventeen-year-old student nurse and married her a year later despite opposition from both sets of parents. Still not yet twenty, he had become a father; was ideally happy with his young wife and baby son when Pamela, his wife, had been killed in a car accident with her parents. His little boy was with Jimmy's parents that day. They looked after Peter, and the boy, now ten years old, was so settled with his grandparents, Jimmy had decided not to attempt to disturb him by trying to set up a home for them both.

It was obvious Jimmy adored the boy and was a devoted, if part-time, father. As a busy resident doctor he could only be with Peter at intervals.

I, in turn, told Jimmy about Tristan's Folly and Father and Jolly but could not bring myself to state more than a few bare facts about Greg as the childhood friend I had always wanted to marry. If Jimmy surmised that I was none too happy now that my wish had been granted, he neither remarked on it nor questioned me about my relationship with my husband.

We remained at the hotel for dinner, a meal Jimmy chose with care and good taste. I found him easy and relaxing to be with, and our evening, despite any earlier misgivings, was a great success.

"We must do this more often!" Jimmy said, smiling, as he drove me back to the hospital. "It's been lovely for me. And, I hope, a break for you."

I wondered if he would try to kiss me good night when he stopped the car outside the nurses' quarters. But he merely pressed my hand and said again: "I *have* enjoyed the evening. Thanks again for coming with me, Samantha!" Then with a wave, he drove off toward the main building.

Peggy was still awake when I went into the bedroom we shared. She gave me a sleepy grin and said:

"Judging by the look on your face, you've had a good time. Naughty girl!"

I felt suddenly miserable. I had, in fact, done nothing that could possibly be construed as 'naughty,' except that I had very much enjoyed the company of an attractive man who was not my husband. I decided the most sensible way to deal with this ridiculous feeling of guilt was to write and tell Greg all about my date. But in the morning I changed my mind. I did not want Greg to think that I was trying to pay him back in his own coin.

Besides, I had every intention of going out with Jimmy again.

12

"Yes, of course you can go!" Matron said sympathetically. "You're due some time off but, as you know, we've been so short staffed I simply couldn't spare you before!"

I breathed a sigh of relief. Father's telephone call telling me Greg had come home on sick leave following a bad bout of 'flu had kept me on tenterhooks all morning while I waited for a chance to see Matron. The hospital had been so lenient about the way they had taken me back after my long absence I did not want to ask for favours. Yet I felt I must go back and nurse Greg. According to Father he was still far from well.

I caught the afternoon bus to the village and walked down the hill to Trevellyan Hall, regretting that William was not with me to enjoy the soft air and sweet-smelling grass. The garden glowed with Aunt Tibby's crimson and yellow tulips. The roses were a blaze of colour against the background of trees.

I went straight to the house, thinking that Greg would have been ordered to bed by

Aunt Tibby. But she told me that he had insisted on going to the flat. She looked worried.

"He's so thin!" she told me. "I told him you were coming on leave the moment I got your call, and he's looking forward to seeing you. So run along, my dear. You don't have to waste precious time being polite to me."

Despite her warning as to Greg's appearance, I was quite unprepared for the sight of him when I opened the door of our sitting room. As he struggled out of the armchair, he seemed to be all arms and legs, and his extreme thinness made him look taller than ever. His face was chalk white, and there were deep, dark shadows under his eyes. They were sunken and lustreless.

He tried to smile, but to me it looked more of a grimace. He dropped back into the armchair with an apology.

"Sorry!" he said. "I still seem to be a bit rickety on my pins." This, from Greg who always minimized pain and illness! I ran to him and dropped to my knees by his chair, covering his hands with mine. His hands were cold.

"Darling, I'm going to light the fire. You're frozen!"

I made as if to do so, but his fingers caught my arms and held me. He looked into my face without speaking, his eyes searching mine as if he were trying to read my thoughts. I felt suddenly shy.

"I'm awfully glad you could get leave!" he said, still holding me. "This damned 'flu makes one so depressed. I feel better already just seeing you. You look well."

"I'm fine! But you are not, Greg. I'm surprised they let you come home in this condition. You obviously weren't fit to travel."

"No, Nurse! Whatever you say, Nurse!"

We were suddenly smiling. I released myself and got busy lighting the fire. Greg made no move to help me. Normally he insisted on carrying the basket of logs, which he thought too heavy for me. He leaned back in his chair, legs outstretched, watching me. No matter what I did or where I went, he watched. It made me nervous and consequently clumsy. I nearly dropped the tea tray when I carried it from the kitchen.

"It's your fault!" I said childishly. "You make me awkward when you stare like that."

His gaze still on me, he said quietly:

"I can't help it. You look so beautiful. I'd forgotten how attractive you are."

I blushed. This was an entirely new role for us. We were like strangers meeting and falling in love for the first time.

"And even prettier with that colour in your cheeks!" he added.

Now he was teasing me, and I recognized the old Greg of happier days. I relaxed and began to pour out the tea.

"I wish *you* had some colour! You're like a scarecrow, Greg. Don't they feed you in that place of yours?"

"Food's quite good," Greg said. "I've just not had much appetite. You cook something for me, Samantha. Then maybe I'll eat it."

"Aunt Tibby is making a chicken fricassee for you," I said. "So I can't cook for you tonight. But as it's one of your favourite dishes, I hope to see you eat a decent meal."

But when the time came, Greg only toyed with his food. As soon as I had washed the dishes, I took him back to the flat. Despite his protests, I insisted he should go to bed.

Once there, he gave up trying to pretend he felt well and finally admitted that he thought he had not completely ousted the influenza bug.

"Or maybe the bug just hung around in order to get a quick look at you, my lovely Samantha!" he said, his eyes teasing, but love in his voice.

I took his hand and held it in mine. It felt

so thin I nearly wept. How could he have lost so much weight in so short a time?

Then I remembered that Jolly had told me how tough a time Greg's fellow officers were giving him. Poor Greg! He must have suffered very severely for it to have taken such a toll of his health.

"Don't look so worried, darling!" he said. "I expect I was overworking. I'll be fine in a day or two."

I went out to the kitchen to fill a hot-water bottle for him. By the time I returned, he was asleep. I slipped the covered bottle near his feet and sat down by the bed.

Asleep, Greg looked utterly defenceless, like a small boy who had been thoroughly beaten in a fight. I gave up struggling to pretend I didn't care. No matter what he had done, I still cared desperately, and I hated to see him like this. I decided there and then that no matter what happened in the future, I would make myself forget the other woman and forget the past until he was well again. With my care he would soon get well.

But it was over a week before Greg showed real signs of recovery, and before that he went down with a fever and the 'flu again. This bug or virus was even more virulent than the first. Old Dr. Edwards was obviously concerned and said that if I hadn't been a student nurse and capable of looking after my husband, he might well have considered sending Greg off to the hospital. But he stayed, and I nursed him day and night.

He was very weak when finally he got up and began to walk around a little. We were fortunate: the weather was mild and sunny. As Greg's recuperation progressed, we went for strolls along the beach. The salt air and bright sunshine finally put some colour back into his face.

I went to visit Father, half hoping he would soften toward Greg in view of his illness and invite him back to the Folly. But although Father sent Greg best wishes for his recovery, his attitude had clearly not changed. He still did not want Greg in his home.

I took William back to the flat with me, knowing his lively, affectionate manner would help to cheer Greg up.

Our personal relationship was loving without being intimate. We called one another 'darling', spoke to each other tenderly, and were thoughtful and gentle with one another. But we were never passionate, and when Greg kissed me, it was always a gentle touch of his lips against my cheek, like that of a platonic friend. As his health improved and he became stronger and more his old self, I found myself wondering how he could maintain this extraordinary restraint. It was unnatural, and a great strain on me, too. There were moments when all my old passionate need of him returned in such force that I longed for him to show some positive reaction to my presence. I wanted him to insist that I sleep with him; to force me to submit to his passion; to *make* me make love with him. But at other times I was grateful he kept his distance between us. I even, on one occasion, tried to pick a quarrel with him over some meaningless thing hoping at least to rouse his anger. Then we might have had a real row, and I could have ended in his arms! But Greg deliberately or unconsciously kept me at arm's length, and although we appeared to be inseparable for the whole of his sick leave, we were never really together.

On his last night in the flat Greg asked me if I'd like to go into Newquay for a drink, to dine, if I chose, and perhaps dance.

"You need a break, darling," he said. "Say what you would like to do and I'll arrange it."

I was reminded of Jimmy Planter using nearly those very words. Once again I was tempted to tell Greg about my evening out with Jimmy. But I did not want anything to mar our last evening together, so I opted to go to Truro instead of Newquay, have a meal there and see a film about the life of Winston Churchill that we'd both not yet seen.

We went by bus and returned in a taxi, holding hands in the back seat like adolescents. We were both silent, and I became very aware of Greg's shoulder touching mine. I was certain he was equally aware of my nearness. I knew then that we would make love when we got home. Deliberately I did not question whether it would be right or wrong. I wanted him just as badly as he wanted me, and beyond that I would not let myself think. This was no time to remember Jane Swan. She had no place here between us in the darkness of the taxi speeding us along the coast road toward Tristan's Bay and home.

Even now, when I have nothing more to believe in or hope for, I'd like to think that that night was the result of genuine love, not simply the bodily hunger of two healthy young people. At the time no one could have convinced me that Greg made love to me without love. He was everything any woman could have wanted in a lover, and I responded with equal tenderness and passion. The only words either of us spoke were words of love, and it seemed to me that we reached new heights, new understanding, were more totally fulfilled in body and spirit than ever before.

I woke next morning in the same exalted mood only to find that Greg had retreated once more into himself. Silent, brooding, inscrutable, and with those same invisible barriers that I had hoped last night were down for good. I, too, retreated, allowing my pride to assert itself and my intense emotion to be superseded by the simple logic that I would be mad ever to trust Greg or believe in him again. I felt cheapened, cheated, and in despair.

Breakfast was barely finished and cleared away before I found myself proved all too right in not trusting Greg after all.

I had supposed his leave was up when he had told me he had to leave early that morning I was astonished, therefore, when he told me suddenly, without warning, that he was catching the mid-morning train from Newquay to London.

"London?" I echoed as if it was the end of the world. "But I thought you were due back at Trenoun?"

Greg stacked the last of the dishes in the plate rack, avoiding my startled gaze.

"I never said that — only that I would

211

be leaving early this morning. I have to go to London for an appointment late this afternoon."

The obvious question froze on my lips. Greg must be going to meet Jane Swan in town because he could no longer be seen with her in Cornwall. I was staggered. I could hardly believe it. After all the apologies and promises and assurances that the affair was over. After last night . . .

Greg must have noticed my taut white face and clenched hands, for he said quietly:

"I'm not meeting Jane, if that's what's worrying you, Sam!"

I breathed again but couldn't be sure if this was the truth. He had lied before. Why not now? Yet his tone was convincing. I held onto my self-control and said quietly:

"Then perhaps you can tell me about your 'appointment.' Who it is with — and where?"

I met with a total silence. My heart sank. We were back once more in the old damnable bog of mystery and misunderstanding. Did Greg have no idea at all how this secretiveness upset me? Unnerved me?

For a moment he did not reply. Then turning away from me he said:

"I have to see my lawyer. Does that satisfy you?"

I knew he was lying by the way he refused to look at me.

"I don't believe you!"

Greg's eyes were bitter as now he did look at me.

"You just can't trust me, can you?" he said.

"No, I don't. I can't. I won't!" I said hysterically. Only a few hours ago I had truly believed that we were reconciled; about to begin a new phase of our life together. I had given him all the love I was capable of without restraint. I had been idiot enough to lay my head on the block.

Greg had packed the night before. I stared incredulously as he began putting his last bits and pieces into the case. He made no move to touch me, no effort to try to put things right.

"I'll just run over to the Hall and say goodbye to Aunt Tibby. Then I must be off. I don't expect you to come to the bus stop with me. I'll be back in a moment or two to get my suitcase."

I let him go. Only when I was alone did I sit down on the bed, my head between my hands, and give way to despair. I could not cry. I was beyond that. My disappointment and hurt were too great for tears. I felt utterly desolate.

213

Pride rescued me. I was determined not to let Greg see how deeply upset I was. When he returned to pick up his case, I was busy packing my own clothes for my return that afternoon to the hospital.

"I'm off now, Sam. I'll have to hurry!" I did no more than nod and continue with my packing. It seemed a long time before I heard the door close quietly behind him. I think he had been waiting for me to succumb as usual in my stupid softhearted way and show him that I still loved and believed in him. I felt a cruel satisfaction that he had had to leave this time without my show of tears or yearning kiss. I hoped he was as miserable and unhappy as I was. But once the flat was empty, my anger evaporated. I stood still, staring at the closed door, wondering if it would open, if Greg would come back. But he didn't.

For a little while after he left, I was able to occupy myself with cleaning the flat before I shut it up and handed the key back to Aunt Tibby. But when there was nothing more to be done and the rooms were spotless and unbearably neat, I could no longer shut my mind to my terrible misgivings about the future. It seemed to me as I sat at the kitchen table idly fondling William's silky ears that I might never come to this little place again. This time I must face up to the fact that my marriage to Greg was a failure if we could not communicate with one another. Greg could not possibly expect me to trust him all over again. The last time I had tried hard to do so, it had ended with his confession of guilt. If trusting him simply meant ignoring truth until he owned up to yet another sordid little secret, I wanted no part in it. It wasn't a life. It would amount to a living death in which I'd be left to imagine all kinds of terrible things, only in the end to have them confirmed.

I tried to see the situation in an unbiased light, as if I were not Greg's wife and it was some other woman sitting at the table asking me if I thought she was being unfair to her husband. But the answers remained the same. I was not being unjust to Greg. It was he who was deceiving me. It was painfully obvious that his trip to London had been planned beforehand, that he had deliberately not told me about it until today. Had I known I would never have encouraged or desired the love-making we had shared the previous night. Bitterly I reflected that the only thing Greg seemed willing to share with me was his body, and even that was not exclusively mine. He could not fail to realize that his 'last minute' trip to London would arouse my suspicions.

Yet why tell me at all?

I knew the answer to that even as the thought flashed across my mind. I had told him at breakfast that I would go to Newquay with him, therefore I would have seen him buy his ticket for Paddington, not for the Trenoun train. But for this he might never have told me he was going to London instead of spending his last day's leave with me.

The idea of Greg working out carefully how best to deceive me was so obnoxious it made me feel physically sick. I found myself thinking that throughout literature there were endless stories of the most charming and handsome of men who finally revealed themselves as scoundrels. Rakes and cheats rarely look like rakes and cheats. In fiction and in real life, too, the villain was so often more attractive than the hero. And still women loved them . . .

Did I still love Greg? I did not know. Did I want to divorce him? I did not know that, either.

I took William across to the Hall. Aunt Tibby made me coffee and talked, as she so often did, about Greg. For once I found the fond, flattering way in which she described him intensely irritating. I wanted to shout at her: "Don't you know what he is *really* like? Are you just pretending to yourself and to me that he is perfect because you don't want to admit he isn't? Or don't you really know about the flaws in his character? He's a liar. He's a cheat. He's an adulterer. And I can prove it to you." But I said nothing. Cold and sick at heart, I made an excuse to leave her.

I hurried away as quickly as I could, before my hysteria got the better of me. Case in hand, I took William across the sand dunes, back home to Tristan's Folly.

I found Father mixing cement on the terrace. I was surprised to see the sun shining. I had not noticed it.

"Back again?" he greeted me teasingly. "It's nice to see my Bad Penny turning up once more."

I sat down on the white-painted iron garden seat and watched him work. He had always enjoyed this kind of job, and he used his spade easily and rhythmically. His actions were somehow soothing to me, and I felt the turmoil within me subside a little. Father seemed not to notice my suitcase. Perhaps he thought I was quiet because I was sad that Greg had gone. I did not feel able to tell him the truth. In any event, what could I say? Nothing, except that it looked as if we had helped the navy to keep someone who was as irresponsible and unreliable as they had suspected before Father and I spoke up for him!

During lunch I felt calmer. Harder, too. This time I was not going to let myself break down. Greg must be nearing London, and if he was keeping a date with another woman, I was not going to let myself care. Sooner or later I would learn the whole truth, and after that I could decide what to do with my life. Meanwhile, I had work to do at the hospital. I had exceeded my leave. It would be up to me to try to make up for my absence, and I would obviously have to study longer and harder in order to catch up before my exams.

So I went back and threw myself headlong into my work. I did not permit myself to dwell on the agonizing thought of Greg or think of anyone or anything outside my life in the hospital.

Occasionally I ran into Jimmy Planter. Whenever he saw me, he was obviously pleased and eager to talk. He invariably invited me out to dinner or for a drink. But I said, truthfully, that I was far too busy.

I think my roommate, Peggy, guessed that all was not well between my husband and myself. I shut her up rather sharply every time she mentioned his name or showed curiosity about my marriage. Finally she took the hint and stopped talking about him.

He wrote to me, letters I very often left on my dressing table unread until the following day. These letters were very matter-of-fact. He never once referred to his trip to London or to that last night of our leave, although he thanked me for taking such good care of him and gave me all the credit for his being fit again and able to work as hard as needed. I had no idea when he might next be home.

Jolly too, wrote to me. He told me that Greg had yet again come an easy first in the exams, and that although most people still avoided his company in the wardroom, they no longer kept him in complete coventry. Jolly thought that, given time, they might accept Greg back entirely. He, himself, had approached Greg once or twice but had been quietly but clearly rebuffed.

Seems he doesn't want to know me now! I suppose, despite what he said, he felt badly about the way I cut him when the heat was on. I'm sorry about it all, but I hope old Father Time will smooth things over eventually.

Although I knew from this letter that Jolly was none too happy about this relationship with Greg, I was glad of it. If Greg were going to end up in trouble a second time, I did not want my brother to be involved.

I had great difficulty in writing to Greg. The few letters I sent were brief accounts of my day-to-day doings. I could not bring myself to write anything personal nor even sign them with love. My emotions were in limbo. I did not know what I felt.

Three weeks passed since my leave, and I was sick of the sight and smell of the hospital. I decided to go out again with Jimmy Planter. I needed a break, and Jimmy offered it to me. I did not realize how susceptible I would become to his quiet sympathy, in particular to his tactful way of handling the situation. He knew I was unhappy and that my marriage was in a precarious state and could so easily have supposed that under such circumstances I might possibly be caught on the rebound. But he never once forced the pace. I let him hold my hand because I found it warm and comforting, reassuring.

But in those early days of our friendship, I did not want him to kiss me; perhaps sensing this, he did not try. However, as our meetings became more frequent and my respect and liking for him increased, my feelings toward him changed.

One night, when he had taken me to a particularly poignant film that left me in an emotional frame of mind, I found myself wondering, if there had been no Greg in my life, whether I might not have fallen in love with Jimmy. Although he was ten years older than I, this disparity in our ages suited me very well. Jimmy tended more and more to take the lead, and I found it restful to sit back and follow. I liked being looked after, treated as if I were a delicate, fragile, valuable object in need of care and protection! It was something I had lacked during my teens with Greg and Jolly treating me either as another boy or, if I behaved in too feminine a way, as a silly girl not fit to share their lives.

I sat beside Jimmy in the dark intimacy of his car as he drove me back toward the hospital and knew that I wanted him to kiss me. I was lonely and bitter and more than a little lost. Jimmy inspired my trust, and I felt that to be held in his arms would be immensely comforting.

With his usual sensitivity, Jimmy perceived my mood, and as he parked the car outside the nurse's home, he put his arms around me as if it were the most natural thing in the world.

I shut my eyes, willing myself not to think of Greg. And for a moment or two, as Jimmy's mouth came down on mine, I found myself responding. His arms tightened around me, and instinctively my own went round his neck. I was trembling and strangely excited. But the moment did not last. Agonizingly, I remembered Greg's kisses, Greg's body, and involuntarily I stiffened.

Immediately, Jimmy released me. I felt like weeping, but he said quietly:

"Don't ever feel you have to do anything you don't wish, Samantha. I take you out because I love being with you, and I think, and hope, you enjoy our evenings together as much as I do. You don't owe me anything. Do you understand?"

I knew very well what he meant. I did not have to kiss him as a duty.

Suddenly, I found myself telling him about my relationship with Greg. I no longer felt it would be disloyal to Greg to do so; moreover, I did owe Jimmy the truth.

I suppose I knew he was falling in love with me. I did not want to admit it to myself because then I would have felt obliged to stop seeing him. I was certainly not in love with him, although I was growing very, very fond of him. I thought if I told him about Greg, he would at least know that I still hoped, however improbable it might be, that my marriage eventually would somehow work out.

Jimmy heard me through to the end, and I was grateful that he refrained from any adverse remarks about Greg. He told me that he, too, had once felt that real love happened only once in a lifetime. When his young wife died, he'd genuinely believed that he would never want to marry again.

"Now I feel otherwise!" he said quietly. "I'm often very lonely. I want a home of my own again, a woman of my own. I want to see more of Peter; to have him to share my life and myself. I would like to get married again. A few years ago I would have said such a thing was impossible. So even if your marriage does break up, it won't mean the end of all chance of happiness for you."

Once again I deliberately played the ostrich and buried my head in the sand. I did not want Jimmy to say that I was the woman who had succeeded in changing his mind about marrying again. I selfishly ignored the implication and asked Jimmy if he believed a platonic friendship was possible between man and woman and between us in particular.

"If it is what *you* want, then we'll make it possible!" Jimmy said. "But don't worry about it, Samantha. Things have a way of working themselves out; meanwhile, let's just enjoy being friends, shall we?"

He made it so easy for me. Perhaps he was old enough and wise enough to realize that this was really all I wanted from him for the moment, that anything more would have put a stop to our evenings out.

I decided to invite him home to the Folly to meet Father. I think Father liked him well enough, but I saw him frowning at lunch when Jimmy made some comment about my preference for white wine to red and, toward the end of the meal, to my weakness for Stilton cheese. It was obvious that Jimmy knew me very well and had made a careful study of my likes and dislikes. Before Jimmy and I returned to the hospital, Father engineered a few moments alone with me and said:

"I like your doctor very much, my dear, but — forgive me if I seem to be interfering in what is not my business — I am a little worried. Greg has hurt you and, I have to say this, turned out a bit of a disappointment to you, to all of us. But you *are* still his wife, and though this may sound a little old-fashioned, it wouldn't be right if . . . "

I broke in quickly:

"There's nothing to worry about, Father. Jimmy and I are genuinely good friends — that's all. I like him very much and enjoy his company, but I'm not having a flirtation with him. I'm not on the rebound or trying to punish Greg."

Father did not return my smile.

"I'm sure you believe that, Sam, but it isn't always easy to see what is really motivating our behaviour. As for Doctor Planter, I think he may not feel quite as platonic towards you as you say you are towards him. I don't say he'd step out of line easily — he strikes me as a very decent fellow. But he's only human, and you could hurt him, my dear. I don't think you quite realize what a beauty you've turned into."

"Oh, Father!" I protested. "You've got your rose-colored spectacles on. I'm not even pretty!"

"You are these days, Sam. More than pretty. Since you lost that thin, haggard look and have filled out, you've blossomed out of all recognition. You're almost as beautiful as your mother was when I first met her."

I was astonished. For Father to make any such remark! I, too, recognized my likeness to my mother from her portrait, but I could never see myself as beautiful, even though Greg had often told me so since our marriage. I thought of myself as ordinary. Jolly and Greg had seen to it when I was in my teens that I never became vain!

As Jimmy drove me back to Newquay, I sat silently beside him, remembering those early days. How simple and easy and happy they had been, even though Greg had not loved me then. It seemed tragic that now, when I was actually his wife, I was so utterly miserable. I wanted the hero of my childhood back. I wanted to be without jealousy, bitterness, hardness, or malice. I hated myself almost as much as I hated Greg, and I blamed him for this unwelcome, ugly change in me. I might look beautiful to Father, perhaps even to Jimmy, but I certainly did not feel it.

Perhaps because I was too greatly reminded of the unhappy state of my marriage by the visit to Tristan's Folly, I clung to Jimmy when later that night he kissed me good night. I forgot my determination to keep our friendship platonic, forgot Father's warnings. I did not anticipate Jimmy's reaction. He tightened his arms around me and I heard his voice — vibrant, husky — against the top of my head.

"Samantha, Samantha, that's the first time you've ever shown any kind of response to my kisses! Tell me it means you're beginning to want more from me than friendship!"

I drew away from him as quickly as if I had been stung, stammering out a stupid apology and then apologizing for the apology. Jimmy interrupted me.

"Don't ever be sorry for what you do or say if it's truly what you think and feel!" he said quietly. "In the long run, you know, honesty is nearly always the kindest as well as the best policy. It is certainly vital between real friends. And we are real friends, aren't we, Samantha?"

He began to stroke my cheek, my hair, gently, without passion. His understanding, his kindness, his goodness, reduced me to nervous weeping. Jimmy let me sob against his shoulder for a few minutes; then, true to form, he produced the proverbial clean handkerchief, made me blow my nose and dry my eyes, and only then suggested we should talk.

"I'm sure I don't need to tell you I'm very much in love with you," he said in the same quiet voice he might have used to announce a weather report. "Any more than you need to tell me you are not in the least in love with me. But I suppose I've been hoping that if your marriage doesn't work out, in the long run you might turn to me. In a way, that is what happened when you kissed me just now. I know quite well it isn't me you need, it's Greg. You're still in love with him, aren't you?"

13

Jimmy gave me time to recover equilibrium. He also gave me food for reflection. I knew every word he spoke was true, including his assumption that I still loved Greg. I might no longer be starry-eyed 'in love,' but I loved him enough not to want any other man in my life, not even someone as nice as Jimmy.

"I suppose I've been trying to fall out of love with Greg. But I don't seem to be able to do it. I don't want to love him. It — it hurts too much." My voice trembled, but I steadied it and went on: "Perhaps I've loved him too long and too much to be able to write him off as a big mistake. Perhaps it will come to that one day, but not yet." I looked at Jimmy in the half darkness of the car, hating myself for hurting him. He looked sad but calm.

"I really mean this, Samantha," he said quietly. "I *hope* it does work out. I want to see you happy. You were laughing, you know, that first day I saw you in the Children's Ward, and I was fascinated. You are even more beautiful when you laugh or smile. I just wish I had the power to bring about such a transformation."

It was on the tip of my tongue to repeat my apology, but remembering what he had said, I refrained. Jimmy smiled at me.

"I know what you're thinking. But no regrets! I'm not in the least sorry I fell in love with you. Even if I never see you again after tonight, I've had so much happiness with you these last weeks, it's been worthwhile. I'm alive again — really emotionally involved once more with another human being. That's good. Not just for me but for my patients, too, I imagine. A 'dead' doctor can't be a good one."

"You, dead!" I argued hotly. "You're a wonderful doctor, Jimmy, and you know it. The patients adore you, and you're incredibly kind and understanding with them. All the nurses agree with me, and Peggy says . . . " I broke off, suddenly embarrassed. But Jimmy would not let me off this so lightly.

"Says what?" he prompted. "Come on, Samantha, put me wise!"

"All right, I will. Peggy says she actually knows a couple of the nurses are in love with you. Don't you realize you're rated Number One Pin-up boy in the hospital?"

Jimmy laughed.

"Really, Samantha, you nurses!" he said.

"Teenyboppers!" But he looked pleased as well as amused.

"They aren't all kids!" I reminded him. "Peggy is my age, for one, and she's green with envy every time you take me out."

Jimmy raised his eyebrows.

"Is that the blonde girl you share a room with? Nurse Dickenson, isn't she?"

I nodded.

"I know. Pretty girl. Maybe when you've had enough of my company, I'll ask her for a date."

But before I could clearly formulate the thought that maybe I should stop seeing Jimmy and leave the field free for girls like Peggy, Jimmy added:

"And don't get any ideas about doing the noble thing and ruining our friendship for my sake or Peggy Dickenson's. So long as you are around the hospital, Samantha, I'm just not interested in her or anyone else. I state that categorically. I'm in love with you, and that you don't and probably never will love me is understood. But for heaven's sake don't run away from me. I need your friendship and any affection you care to give me."

"But, Jimmy . . . "

"I mean it. I'm no raw boy, Samantha, who doesn't know what's good or bad for him. I know what I'm doing, and my eyes are wide open. I'm fully prepared to hear you're reconciled with your Greg, and if that's what you want and it will make you happy, I'll do anything possible to hurry on the day. So let me help if I can. It *is* what you want, isn't it?"

I felt a lump in my throat. His brown eyes were full of tenderness. I said, "Yes, it's what I want, but I'm not sure it's possible."

Jimmy lifted his brows, took one of my hands and looked at it speculatively.

"Samantha, you're a sensible girl and an intelligent one, and you're not the sort of person who would be spiteful or stop caring about somebody just because they did something wrong. Surely you can forgive your husband?"

I drew my hand away. I didn't look at Jimmy.

"I would forgive him. I *did*, but . . . "

"He has let you down again?"

"I don't know. I think so. I suppose I ought to trust him, believe in him again, but I . . . *can't!*"

Jimmy nodded. He looked troubled as he said quietly:

"Try and keep your faith, Samantha. Even if a man's done something wrong he must be able to hope his wife will stand by him and believe in him. If not the woman who loves him, who else?"

He almost made me feel ashamed of myself. I thought him wonderful, feeling as he did about me, to give Greg the benefit of the doubt. It heightened my liking for Jimmy, and it was on that night that I began to feel more than ordinary friendship for him — to feel a growing love, based on affection and respect.

When I was alone and thought it all over, I felt confused and wretchedly unsure of myself. I was torn between two men now: Greg, the man I loved and had married, but who had hurt me so abominably, and Jimmy, the lighthouse that kept me from being wrecked in the waters that raged around me. I felt I ought not to lose faith in Greg. I tried to make new allowances for Greg's inexplicable behaviour, mainly because Jimmy thought that I should.

That night I wrote to Greg in very different terms from those in my previous letters. I told him that I thought it was time we tried to arrange another leave together; that I hoped if we did so, we could resolve the uncertainties that had spoiled the end of our last leave. I ended by declaring my love for him in simple terms:

I love you very much, Greg, and I am missing you more than I can say. Please let's see each other soon, darling.

The swift reply I had expected did not arrive. It was almost a week before Greg answered. He could not get leave, he said. As far as the explanations I felt so vital to our relationship, he would not be able to supply them. Nevertheless, he did love me. He was so happy to know I still loved him in spite of everything. I was to take good care of myself, write often, and go on trusting him as much as I could.

A letter from Jolly also arrived, making me welcome Greg's news that he could not get home to see me. Jolly's letter was badly written, obviously penned with considerable emotion in which bitterness predominated.

I don't know how to put this in a way that isn't going to upset you terribly. I've been through hours of torment wondering whether to tell you or not, but I really don't think I can continue to remain silent while Greg is making a fool of you. He told me last night that he had had a letter from you asking him to try to get leave, and since he could not do so, he hoped I could get home for a few days to cheer you up. It's a marvel I did not hit him for his effrontery.

Sam, the reason he can't get leave is because he's already had it. He has had two forty-eight hour passes since his sick leave, and I happen to know each time he went to London.

What I cannot understand is that he must know I know what he's up to, yet he offers no explanation. At least he doesn't have the gall to ask me not to let on to you that he doesn't go home on his leaves. But he must realize I feel obligated to keep you informed for your sake.

The first time he went up to town I gave him the benefit of the doubt. After all, he could have been going to see the dentist or a solicitor or a sick friend or whatever. But to go again two weeks later . . . well, it's as if he hadn't got a wife who would want to share his leaves with him.

I'm just hoping that he may have written to tell you what he's up to and that you can write and tell me to stop trying to upset your apple cart a second time. I would welcome your criticisms but can't somehow believe it will arrive by the next post.

Greg is different. He simply is not the Greg we knew, even allowing for the somewhat difficult time he has had here since the last upheaval. He has become completely antisocial and rejects any attempts on my part to be friendly. It's as if he particularly wants to keep me at arm's length. This from my best friend, my brother-in-law. It doesn't make sense.

I think you should come here and have it out with Greg. The odd thing is, when he talks of you, he still sounds as if he's as keen on you as ever. I hope you understand because I do not, and my old affection for him is rapidly wearing very thin indeed. I really would want to kill him if he hurt you again.

Let me know if you can come here, and I'll arrange a hotel room etc, for you.

All my love,
Jolly

I felt physically sick as I put down his letter. Jolly probably did not know, as I did, that Greg had in fact made three trips to London, counting the one he made the last day of his sick leave. I read Jolly's letter a second time. I wondered if Greg really had been going to see a lawyer. Perhaps Jane Swan's husband was starting divorce proceedings. But I knew this could not be the answer. Greg could have told me if this were the case. I would have been sympathetic and helpful.

I had a crazy idea that I might hire a private detective to shadow Greg, but that sounded so melodramatic I did not give it a second thought. Not then. But a week later, sitting in the lounge of the hotel in Trenoun talking the whole thing over with Jolly and getting exactly nowhere, the thought filtered through my mind again.

"If I had Greg followed, we'd find out exactly what he is up to!" I announced.

Jolly raised his eyebrows.

"Those could be pretty stiff measures, Sam. I mean, apart from the cost, which would be high, I imagine, suppose you did learn the truth, wouldn't it be unacceptable? Would you want to divorce him?"

"Oh, God, I don't know!" I said wretchedly. "Greg begged me to trust him. He did so even before I married him — as if he knew all this was going to happen."

"All what?"

"All this mystery!" I retorted sharply. "Whenever we've talked about it, it has always ended with Greg's refusal to enlighten me and his demand; *"Trust me"* I'd hardly be doing that if I put a detective on him. Yet I can't go on like this. Doesn't he have any idea what he is doing to me?"

Jolly looked miserable.

"I expect Father would pay for your detective, though on second thoughts I don't think he'd like the idea of you ferreting out Greg's private business."

"Neither do I!" I said. "Maybe we'll drop that idea. It's rather horrible, and I don't know why I thought of it in the first place. If only Greg would tell me himself what is going on!"

Jolly sighed.

"I understand: you feel driven to any lengths, Sam. But if not a detective, what *are* you going to do?"

"Have one last talk with Greg!" I said. "I'll give him a final chance to be honest with me."

I had arranged for my brother to meet my train and take me to the hotel at least an hour before Greg expected me to arrive to give us a chance to talk things over before I had to face Greg. I asked Jolly to leave before Greg was due at the hotel. Then I went up to my room, made up my face, and changed into white slacks and a jersey. I stared critically at myself in the mirror. I was startled to see how young I looked with my hair hanging loose on my shoulders. Impatiently I piled it up on top of my head, securing it with pins and was gratified that it added at least five years to my appearance. I wanted to impress on Greg that I was mature enough, sophisticated enough, to stand side by side with him if he was in any trouble, that if this silence of his was designed to protect me, it was a wrong tactic and that I could help him deal with anything, once I knew the facts.

But when Greg came into the room, I instantly shed those five years I had so carefully added. My heart thudded, my hands and legs trembled, and my throat went dry. After all these weeks, here in the doorway was my husband, the man I loved, Greg.

I flung myself into his open arms. All I could say was "Darling, darling!" over and over again.

He kissed me, held me at arm's length while he looked at me in an intent way, kissed me again, and then hugged me with a fierceness he had rarely shown.

"I can't believe you're here — really here!" he said, his voice husky. "I've missed you so damn much I thought I'd go out of my mind. I love you, darling. You're so beautiful! More beautiful today than ever, I think. Let me look at you!"

Even as I stood back, self-conscious, shy, flattered by his praise, a tiny warning shock sparked through my brain. Greg had missed me so much, but not enough to want to spend his last two leaves with me.

"Sammy, you are more beautiful than ever. You've put on weight, I think. I like your hair done on top that way. It suits you. Oh, *Sam!*"

He began kissing me again, and I deliberately put out of my mind the reason for my visit, my doubts, my fears, all the questions and answers that had to come, must come later. Not now while I was in his arms. My own love and need for him swamped every other feeling.

I had read in books of lovers 'devouring' each other. Now I understood the meaning. Greg and I were so hungry for each other that we were almost fighting to get closer, ever closer. I remember at one point pushing Greg's hands away from my face so that I could put my own about his. Our clothes lay scattered around the room as if there had been a whirlwind. Indeed, I felt that I was caught up in a vortex from which there was no escape, even had I wished it.

Our lovemaking over, I lay relaxed in his arms.

His voice brought me back to reality.

"I still find it hard to believe you're really here with me," he said, his voice deep, satisfied, and — I could swear — absolutely sincere. "It felt like a hundred years since my sick leave, and I was in despair not knowing when I could next get home again."

With his arms still holding me, his hands caressing me, I could hardly bear the ugly memory that intruded. Finally I said:

"Greg, you've had two forty-eight hour passes since your sick leave, but you didn't come home. Why not?"

I felt his body shudder, and he drew in his breath sharply. I knew to a second how long it was before he let it out in a long deep sigh.

"Because I went to London!"

The way I reacted to that honest answer surprised him, for I twisted around and hugged him once more in a fierce embrace. For a moment nothing mattered to me but that he had not lied again. If he could be this honest, the rest would surely follow.

"Oh, *darling!*" I whispered. "Thank you for telling me. I was so afraid you'd deny it!"

Now it was his reaction that startled me. Easing out of my arms, he reached over me to the bedside table, took a cigarette from the packet, and lit it before replying. When he did so, his whole manner had changed. His voice was rasping and ironic.

240

"I'd be rather a fool to lie about it when Jolly has obviously informed you when and where I went."

All my happiness and exultation vanished. My body seemed suddenly clammy and cold. I reached automatically for my dressing gown in order to cover myself, for I was naked. I felt horribly cold and apprehensive. But I tried to speak casually.

"Greg, you know Jolly was only trying to protect me. After last time, it was natural for him to assume . . ."

"That I was up to my old tricks!" Greg cut in. "Well, I was not. I did not go to meet Jane Swan. I did not go to meet any woman. Will that satisfy you, Sam?"

"No!" My resolve hardened. "Nothing but the whole truth will satisfy me now, Greg. I cannot go on living with you in a kind of permanent fog. Don't you understand?" I appealed to him now from my heart. "I love you, Greg. I love you enough to forgive you anything as long as it is not a repetition of what happened last time. I'm prepared to believe there's no other woman, but if you won't tell me what you were doing, or why it was necessary to spend your leave with anyone but me, I have to suspect the worst. You leave me no alternative."

Greg got out of bed. He, too, began to

dress. I thought he looked deadly tired. I waited for him to reply, but none came.

My heart sank.

"Greg, listen to me, please!" I begged. "If we can't communicate with each other, our marriage is pointless. Do try to understand. I can learn to live with the truth even if I don't like it, but not to know is destroying me."

He did not look at me but turned his back and began to brush his hair.

"I'm sorry, Sam. I've nothing to say."

His voice was adamant.

"You mean you've nothing you *want* to say. Greg, don't shut me out. *Tell me*. Have you been gambling, drinking, or are you in debt?"

I did not really think any of these things likely, but there seemed no other possibility until a thought struck me. "Greg, you aren't ill?" I was suddenly terrified. "Are you ill? Did you go to London to see a doctor and are afraid to tell me because there's something terrible wrong with your health? *Greg!*"

I went to him, caught his arms with both my hands, fear, like ice, freezing out all my other emotions.

He shook his head and moved slowly back from me, but his voice was oddly gentle.

"No, darling. It's not that. I assure you I'm perfectly fit."

My relief evaporated in anger.

"Then for heaven's sake, tell me the truth. Can't you see how you are torturing me?"

Greg turned away from me again so that I could not see his expression, but when he spoke, his voice was cool and unrelenting.

"I have nothing else to say, Samantha. I'm sorry!"

"You aren't! If you really cared how I felt, you'd put an end to all this. You don't know what love means, Greg. A person really in love puts his loved one's happiness before his own." I was thinking of Jimmy Planter as I spoke. Now driven to near hysteria by Greg's indifference, I said; "Perhaps you might be more concerned if I warn you I may not want to carry on with our marriage if this is the way it's going to be all the time. I don't *have* to stay married to you. You've already given me grounds for divorce, and I know someone who would be more than happy if I were free," I added before I could restrain myself.

Now at last I had Greg's attention. He turned to me, his eyes narrowed, his mouth twisted. He was obviously shaken.

"I see! So there's someone else in your life!"

Having roused his jealousy, I was curiously sorry and a little scared of the consequences. But I was not going to back out of it. I, at least, would not keep the truth from Greg.

"Yes, there is — a doctor at the hospital. I happen to like him very much, and he happens to be very much in love with me. But unlike you, I have *not* been unfaithful," I added darkly.

I turned and walked back to the bed, my body shaking with nervous reaction. Greg came close. I could not read his expression but most of the colour had left his face. He really looked grim.

"I'm sure you think I deserve that last remark," he said in a low voice, "and I suppose I should thank you for — for not being as rotten to me as you think I've been to you."

"Oh, Greg!" I said, exasperated. "Don't you understand! Marriage isn't a game where husband and wife try to score off each other, get even with each other. You and I are supposed to be in love, to care what the other feels and needs. It seems as if the only way you and I can achieve this is in bed!"

He flushed, so I knew my sarcasm had affected him, but he ignored my remark.

"Tell me about him," was all he said.

"There's nothing much to tell. He's thirty

plus, a widower with a little boy of ten. He's a very good doctor and an extremely nice person. I'm not in love with him, but I do like him very much."

"And you say he's in love with you. So I assume it's neither a new friendship nor an entirely platonic one. How long has it been going on?

"We've dined together once or twice a week, seen each other fairly regularly during the past month or so. And I took him home on my last day off."

Greg walked away, his back rigid.

"So that's that! I take it you mean to go on with the affair?"

"It isn't an 'affair'! We're very good friends. I told you, I don't love him. Greg, don't you understand I don't want anyone else in my life but you? But if you go on refusing to be honest with me, how can our relationship be any good? It isn't my fault, it's yours." Tears filled my eyes.

"I can't help it!" Greg's voice was strangled. He looked as unhappy as I felt. Suddenly I wished I had not mentioned Jimmy. Yet I had to make Greg understand he could lose me if he refused to be frank with me.

"You *can* help it!" I cried bitterly. "You can prove you really do want our marriage

245

to work, but you're doing the reverse. You're wrecking it. I don't believe you are really interested in us. You didn't even want a family. You didn't mind my losing the baby, did you? If you were honest, and I asked you now to give me another child here tonight, you'd say no, wouldn't you?"

He hesitated only for a second, then answered:

"Yes, I'm afraid I would!"

"Well, fortunately for you, I don't want one," I said harshly. "Not with our marriage in this state, not with you behaving as if I meant no more to you than your — your mistress!"

Suddenly he lunged towards me with his hand lifted. For one awful moment I thought he was going to strike me. His eyes were furious, and his mouth set in an ugly grimace. But at the last instant he regained control of himself. His hand fell to his side. And then he was beside me, holding both my hands, all the ugly harsh lines that made him a total stranger fading from his face.

"Sam, I know it's pointless for me to say this, but please don't leave me. *Not now. Not yet.* Give me more time. I need time. Don't contemplate pushing off with this doctor of yours. Marriage with him wouldn't work. I can't explain, but I know it's the truth. Just as it's true that I do truly love you, honestly. Don't give up now. Go on being patient, and even if you find it difficult to understand, trust me. *Please*, Sam."

I sat on the edge of the bed, still and utterly confused. I wanted to tell Greg I would carry on, but the only words that came out were:

"For how much longer must I be patient, Greg? How much more time do you need?"

He released me. I fancied I could read a kind of hopelessness in his eyes. When he spoke, I knew I was right.

"I can't answer that. I don't know myself."

I wanted to cry, but I could not. I felt angered, cheated, defeated. I said coldly:

"Then I can't tell you how much longer I'm willing to stay married to you."

Greg opened his mouth as if to speak, but whatever words rose to his lips died there. He stood mute, stubbornly so. I felt all my love and longing ebbing, dwindling.

"I was crazy ever to come here today," I said. "I ought to have known I'd get nowhere. I don't seem to learn from bitter experience, do I?"

Now Greg did open his mouth.

"Don't be bitter," he said, his voice quite gentle and to me, unnerving. "It doesn't suit you and it isn't like you, Sam. You have made no mistakes. It is my fault — all of it."

I held back the tears that were threatening again.

"You've said that before, but you don't do anything constructive to put it right."

He nodded.

"I admit all that. You've been wonderful to put up with so much from me, and I've no right to ask you to put up with any more. You must decide what you want to do. Do you want to cut your leave short, Sam, and go home at once?"

In one way I did; in another I did not. I could see for myself that Greg was terribly unhappy and in some sort of fix, and that made me tolerant. I remembered the thrilled and excited way in which he had welcomed me here. I remembered the way he had just made love to me. No matter what else I doubted, I could have no doubt that Greg still wanted me. Passion aside, he needed me with him to give him strength, some sort of moral support. I knew it would tear him in two if I left now. I could not forget Jimmy's words — that a wife must stand by her husband. Yet to stay would be tantamount to accepting Greg's terms, and they had become unbearable.

Unbearable? Not really! I might dislike

them, fear them, fight them, but I could accept them merely by doing nothing. If in doubt, do nothing! It was one of Father's favourite bits of advice. With a long, long sigh, I looked up at Greg.

"How long have you got off duty?" I asked.

"Until classes at nine tomorrow morning."

"I'll stay till then." I said in a low voice and tried not to see the joy that swept across his face. I did not want him to think that yet again he had 'won'. I added quickly: "But I have to get down to some serious thinking about our future. Perhaps you should do that, too, Greg. Then on your next leave we might reach some definite decision about what we intend to do."

"I agree," Greg said. He still looked as if he had been reprieved.

There was nothing whatever to warn me at this moment that only a few weeks from now, I would be back home at Tristan's Folly, sitting in my turret bedroom, trying to work out the easiest and quickest way to get a divorce.

14

I was in the middle of a lecture on blood transfusions when I was summoned to Matron's office. I knew it must be something serious for her to interrupt a class, and I opened the door of her room with a definite sense of foreboding.

"Sit down, my dear!" Her voice was calm, but her eyebrows were drawn together in a frown. "I'm afraid I have rather serious news for you."

I caught my breath. Was Father ill? Had Jolly had a car accident? Was Greg ill again?

"It's about your husband. Your father just telephoned me to say he thinks it best you go home at once, and under the circumstances, I agree."

I looked at Matron, nonplussed. She had still failed to tell me what was wrong.

"Greg — is he ill?"

Matron seemed to be avoiding my eyes. I felt sick. She was usually so matter-of-fact and so direct. Giving people bad news was part of everyday life for her. Why should she be finding this so hard to say?

"Your husband is not ill. I'm afraid he is in some kind of trouble!"

My muscles tightened. I could not understand why Father had confided our private affairs to Matron. It was quite unlike him. I remained silent, my thoughts chaotic. She glanced at me and then away again.

"I'm afraid this may come as a shock to you, my dear, but your husband has been arrested."

My mouth fell open. I stared at her incredulously.

"*What* did you say?" I asked stupidly.

Matron looked even more distressed.

"You might as well know the facts, my dear, and you must be brave. It isn't pleasant. He was arrested in London this morning and is being held on suspicion of selling secret information to a foreign power."

The blood rushed to my face.

"You can't mean that!" I gasped. But my mind had already started to fit the pieces of the jigsaw puzzle into a picture I at last understood — Greg's unexplained visits to London, his secrecy, and the nasty little Mr. Richards.

"Your father thinks this could involve you all in a great deal of publicity once the news leaks out. I understand your brother telephoned the information to your father from his base. He is on his way home, and your father feels it would be best if you, too, went home at once. You know what the press is, and things could become very difficult for you if the reporters start hounding you and your family. I'm so very sorry, my dear, and I'm sure there's no truth in the accusations. All the same, it's very worrying for you."

I was quite speechless. Matron went to her cupboard and came back with a medicine glass with brandy, which she persuaded me to drink. She was obviously embarrassed as well as upset.

"It was a big enough shock to me," she said gently, "so I do understand how you must be feeling. But don't despair. Let us hope things are not quite as bad as your father seems to think."

I wished I could share her optimism. Father and I knew already that Greg was not to be trusted. Matron knew nothing of his earlier disgrace.

"I'm afraid I inadvertently forced Commander Jolland to tell more than he wished. I would never have done so had I for one moment suspected . . . " Her voice trailed away. Then she said more firmly, "When your father asked me to allow you home on leave, I insisted on his giving me a very good reason. You'd already been away on both sick and compassionate leave, and we need you here, and you need to concentrate on your studies."

Matron was the first of many people who would give me that same look of compassion and pity. Later it would begin to irritate me, but at this moment it merely frightened me.

"These things can drag on for some time, even if a man in your husband's position is eventually proved innocent," Matron said. "It would therefore probably be best for you and the hospital if you stay away indefinitely. I'll tell them here you have had bad news. For the moment any further explanation is unnecessary. I'm sorry, my dear. You're a good nurse, and you've been a hard worker. I shall be sorry to see you leave."

I gasped. I realized she was tactfully asking me to resign. It was on the tip of my tongue to protest, to say that *I* had done nothing wrong; I had given the hospital authorities no cause to call for my resignation. But the words died on my lips. I was Greg's wife, and his disgrace must necessarily become mine. It would affect all of us, Father, Jolly, poor Aunt Tibby . . . I put down the empty brandy glass and stood up.

"I understand!" I said. "Thank you for everything you have done for me, Matron."

She came around the desk to put a hand on my shoulder.

"Your husband may be innocent," she said gently. "I know you love him, so I'll pray for you and him. You'll need all your courage in the days ahead. And if he is proved innocent, why of course come back to us."

My courage, however, was at a very low ebb when finally I walked out of the hospital with my suitcase, like a girl who had been expelled from school. There was not even a chance to say goodbye to Peggy, my friend and roommate.

A car drew up beside me and with some surprise, I saw Jimmy leaning across the passenger seat holding open the door for me.

"Going on leave?" he asked. Automatically, in silence, I climbed in. He shut the door. "Lucky I ran into you," he added.

Lucky! I thought bitterly. Would I ever be lucky again? All the same, it was good to be in Jimmy's car and to feel his friendly reassuring hand on mine. I did not know how to tell him what had happened so that he would believe me. It would all sound so fantastic, too melodramatic to be true.

"Something is wrong." Jimmy's quiet voice roused me from my thoughts as we drove out of the hospital grounds onto the main road. "Come along, Samantha. What's it all about?"

Suddenly I found myself telling him everything. I knew that I could trust him absolutely not to repeat anything. By the time we were nearly at Newquay bus station, I finished. Jimmy parked the car before he made any comment. Then he took my hand again and held it firmly.

"You may get home and find this has all been a big mistake. Don't lose heart, Samantha," he said. "Mistakes can be made, you know. You know Greg. Surely you must know in your own heart that he isn't and would not be a traitor."

The word sent a shiver up my spine.

"That is what people are going to call him if it's true," he said gently. "And don't let it frighten you. You know the old saying: Sticks and stones can hurt my bones, but words can hurt me never!"

I tried to return his smile and be cool and optimistic. But I did know Greg — only too well. I knew he was capable of lies, of deceit, of irresponsibility, of immorality. If he could betray me, why not his country?

It was Jimmy who went to the bus station and found out when the next bus to Tristan's Bay was leaving; Jimmy who took me into a restaurant and made me drink strong black coffee, who would have driven me home himself if he wasn't on call at one o'clock. He carried my suitcase onto the bus, held my hand, kissed me goodbye, and said he would phone me that evening. Meanwhile, he insisted I must try not to worry.

"Don't look so . . . so defeated!" he said softly just before the bus moved off. "It won't affect my feelings for you. Remember that, won't you?"

I tried to find some comfort in the thought that I had one good and true friend, as the bus sped me along the familiar road toward home. I thought of Father waiting for me and felt a rush of pity for him. Some of the dirt — and dirt it would be — would be bound to touch him. He was Greg's father-in-law, had personally gone to the Admiralty to vouch for Greg's basic integrity. Greg had betrayed him, too.

For the first time since Matron broke the news to me, I tried to imagine Greg doing the terrible things of which he was accused. Despite everything I could not believe that Greg, the boy I'd known all my life, was a traitor.

But my fears that he was guilty slowly increased as I recalled so many of the mysteries that were now grimly explained; Mr. Richards; the trips to London; his refusal

256

to give me a time limit when we could wipe the slate clean and begin again; his reticence; the way he had evaded all my questions.

I arrived home to find Father talking on the telephone. He was trying to arrange a special lawyer for Greg's defence. I was deeply touched. Then we went into the library, Jolly was sitting on the sofa, dejectedly smoking. He put down the cigarette, stood up, and kissed me on the cheek.

"I don't know why you don't let Greg stew in his own juice!" he said childishly, and scowled at Father. "It's the end as far as I am concerned."

"Unfortunately it's far from the end; it's the beginning," Father sighed and sat down heavily in his chair. "We're all involved, Jolly, and Samantha most of all. She's Greg's wife."

"She should have divorced him months ago!" Jolly said violently. His eyes were utterly miserable. "She should never have married him in the first place. He's — dirty."

"That'll do, Jolly!" Father's voice was sharp. "There'll be quite enough people ready to call him names and believe he's guilty. Remember he hasn't been tried yet, and in this country a man is innocent until proved otherwise."

I wanted to hug him. Father was always

257

the same — always just and fair.

"*You* don't think him innocent!" Jolly said fiercely. "No more than I do. And I bet in her heart, Sam doesn't, either."

"That's not the point, Jolly. The lawyer, Makepeace, will arrive here this evening. He has already seen Greg, and he'll be able to clarify the picture. There's no point in discussion until we hear more of the facts."

Somehow we got through the afternoon. Jolly and I filled in time by taking William for a long walk across the cliffs. Obedient to Father's wishes, we did not discuss Greg, but it was too much on our minds for us to find alternative topics of conversation, so we walked in silence.

I think I kept calm only because I hoped that by some miracle, George Makepeace would bring us good news. Like Father, I intended to make myself believe in my husband's innocence until I could no longer do so.

That moment came all too soon. The solicitor's first words when we sat down together in the library were ominous.

"I'm afraid Greg has been stupid enough to sign a written confession. I warned him not to do this when he first telephoned me to say he had been arrested. But he went against my advice, and his position is now very serious indeed. He'll want a first-class counsel. His defence won't be easy."

"Father has already arranged it," I replied, my voice so calm and level I couldn't believe it was I speaking.

"Yes, I've engaged Sinclair Mellors. You agree he's one of the best for this kind of thing, Makepeace?"

The solicitor nodded.

"How — how was Greg when you saw him?" I was no longer calm. My voice trembled. Mr. Makepeace looked at me pityingly.

"Not too good, I'm afraid. I had the impression that he did not mean to put up any kind of a fight. It was as if — well, as if he knew he was already condemned."

The choice of words was unfortunate, but Father forestalled my frantic question by saying quickly:

"He won't be shot, Samantha, if that's what's worrying you. It'll mean a long term in prison . . . a very long term."

"Of course, there's always the chance the court will be lenient with him — his past record, his youth."

Their voices droned on, calmly saying such terrible things, I shut my ears to them. They were talking now as if Greg had already been convicted; as if he would be in prison for years and years. I might not see him again, or, if and when I did, he might be a broken man. I was sure Greg could not live in the confines of a prison. He was too young, too vital, too full of energy and zest for life. He needed the wide-open spaces, the sun, the sand, and most of all, the sea.

"Jolly, take your sister upstairs and see she goes to bed at once. Stay with her, will you?"

Dimly I heard Father's voice. Vaguely I was aware of Jolly taking my arm and leading me up the twisting staircase to my room. I sat numbly on my bed while he went for Elsie. When the old woman came into my room, she had been crying. Her voice was very gentle, as were her hands when she helped me to undress. Later Jolly returned with a glass of hot milk, and some pills. Then he sat by my bed and held my hand. I tried to apologize, but he stopped me. "You've every reason to be upset," he said. "And before this, there was the accident and your miscarriage." His voice became suddenly husky. "I suppose the way things have turned out, it was just as well you lost your baby, Sam."

I knew he was right, yet I thought I might have been comforted if I had had a child of Greg's to nurse in my arms now.

"Jolly, I still . . . love . . . him!"

"Oh, Sam!" My brother's voice was a mixture of exasperation and affection. "You always were an idiot, especially about Greg. About both of us, really. We treated you pretty badly, yet you always came back for more. You never once held it against us for the way we often ran off and left you, knowing you couldn't run fast enough to catch up with us. I expect we teased you shockingly. And you're still too damned soft and forgiving. That's your trouble."

"But it isn't strictly true!" I argued. "I seem to be able to go on loving, yet I can't forgive Greg — for Jane Swan I mean. And this . . . well, I'll never be able to forgive him this."

Jolly scratched his head.

"It's funny about that woman," he said gruffly, as much to himself as to me. "If she really was a spy working with him, why in heaven's name weren't they more careful? It doesn't make sense."

I looked at him wide-eyed. I had not connected Jane Swan with this new trouble.

"Jolly, if she was buying information from Greg, then maybe they weren't having an affair, and that was simply Greg's cover story."

"Pretty poor cover!" Jolly said with disgust.

261

"I can't believe *she* would have been so obvious even if Greg was green enough to know no better, which I doubt. I don't think she had anything to do with this. I think Greg missed the cash handout when their affair was blown open and resorted to getting money some other way."

"If he did get money, he took care not to let me know about it this time."

"They'll check his bank account, of course, if they haven't already done so. They probably did that before they arrested him. He hasn't been very clever, has he?"

Jolly stopped talking and looked at me anxiously.

"No more talking about Greg, Sam. We'll have plenty of time tomorrow. You try to sleep now."

I felt unnaturally alert, but I wanted suddenly to be alone, so I lied to Jolly and told him I thought if he turned out the light and left me, I would probably sleep.

"Anything you want in the night, give me a shout," he said. "I'll look in again before I go to bed."

I waited until the sound of his footsteps died away. Then I got out of bed and switched on the light. I went across to my desk and pulled out an old exercise book in which, as an adolescent girl, I had scribbled romantic poems full of my unrequited love for Greg. Most of the pages were blank. I tore out the poems, scratched across the cover: 'Diary of Samantha Trevellyan'. I thought if I could put down an account of my life with Greg, see it in black and white, I might begin to understand him and what he had done.

So it was I began this diary.

That was a week ago. Since then we have been hounded by reporters, Intelligence, by well-meaning and not so well-meaning friends. Despite the isolation of Tristan's Folly there has been a procession of callers, talking, asking, consoling, advising, admonishing, pitying, condemning. Father looks twenty years older, and it is Jolly now who is coping with everything. The pressure is beginning to ease a little, but we all know that this is only the lull before the storm when Greg's trial takes place. We may have to endure a repetition of all this unless we go into hiding. And Father has refused to do any such thing.

"This family has done nothing and will do nothing to be ashamed of," he declared at dinner this evening, and his face looked carved of stone. "We will stay here and hold up our heads and preserve the honour of our family. Is that understood?"

Mercifully for her, Aunt Tibby has received less attention. I think that's due to the fact that she steadfastly refused to utter one word other than that she believes her nephew to be innocent. I have visited her several times and she says the same to me.

"My dear Samantha," she said coldly on one occasion, when I tried to kiss her. "I don't need sympathy or pity. Why should I? Greg is innocent."

I dread the day Greg is actually found guilty. But I know that day has to come. I have here on my desk a letter from him telling me so.

I can endure what is happening to me, but the thought of what you must be suffering at home is a constant and unending torture to me. I have to tell you that it will get worse. You see, Samantha, I will be found guilty. It is inevitable.

Perhaps it will horrify you to read this request, but despite all that has happened, all that will happen in the future, I am once again asking you to believe in me; most of all to believe that I love you. I always have, and I always will. I don't expect you to understand, and I suppose it is too much to ask you to go on loving me. I ask only that you should try for a

264

*while to keep faith. The marriage service
says specifically for better or for worse. I
have no right to do so, yet I ask you not to
leave me now. Not yet. I love you truly.*
                                    Greg

So I am trying to make up my mind
whether or not to divorce him. I cannot
forget his letter or rid my mind of the belief
that he does love me and that I am all he
has left. All that is honest, decent, good. He
has no honour of his own, no values left. He
lost them all when he betrayed this country.
I don't need to condemn him because he
has condemned himself. He must have told
so many lies to so many people. Yet I find
myself believing him when he writes, '*I love
you truly.*' It could so easily be another lie.
Yet my heart tells me it is not.

Do I still love Greg? I don't know. I loved
him too much in the past to be able to write
him out of my life now as if he had never
been my husband, my lover, my friend. I
cannot, as Father and Jolly now want me
to, accept that our marriage was empty,
meaningless, and such a mistake that divorce
is the only way out. Yet I am haunted by the
knowledge that it may have to end that way.
But I remember how Greg begged me again
and again to believe in him, to trust him,

265

no matter what the world said about him. I gave him my promise before I married him. I cannot forget that I did so.

I don't know what to do. I would like to see Greg, talk to him. But I have been told he has refused visits from any of his family. I don't know what I would say to him if I did see him. Neither can I find words to write to him.

Now, sitting at my desk, I re-read his letter. I am still no nearer a decision. If only Greg had not begged me to go on believing in him; to keep faith. I no longer have any faith except perhaps that he does love me. *I don't want him to love me.* I don't want to love him.

In my heart of hearts, I know Father and Jolly are right and that the time is fast approaching when I must write and ask Greg to set me free.

15

It was Jimmy, more than anyone else, who helped me get through the next few months. He telephoned two or three times a week, and it gradually became his habit to spend his off-duty time with me. No one could have been a better friend than he was during the ordeal that inevitably followed Greg's arrest.

The date for his trial had still not been fixed. I wanted desperately to see Greg, but he continued to refuse visits from any of the family. He seemed to want to cut himself off from us forever.

I had no idea when I would see him again. This, as much as the weeks of strain and anxiety, finally broke me. I cried ceaselessly for three days. Not even the anxious faces of Father and Jolly, bending over me could stem my tears. Nor could I sleep without Dr. Edwards' pills, and even then I dreamed violent, unhappy dreams from which I woke still crying.

Jimmy took charge. He had a long serious talk with me one afternoon when we were alone. He made me pull myself together, forced me to start thinking of Father and Jolly and poor Aunt Tibby instead of myself. Later I realized his harsh method of treatment was far more effective than the tolerance and sympathy Father and Jolly lavished on me. Gradually I responded to Jimmy's challenge and began to regain a sense of proportion.

Father, as he came to know Jimmy better, liked him. I think he began to hope that I might turn to Jimmy and eventually find happiness in a second marriage. But on my part, I wanted nothing more to do with love after my experience with Greg. I trusted Jimmy, but I did not trust the emotion called love. Life, I decided, would be simpler without it.

As time went on, Jolly also began to appreciate Jimmy more fully. My brother had been posted to Truro, and he settled down there with new colleagues and new work, so he was beginning to put the past behind him. I knew he still felt bitter toward Greg, but he was considerate enough of my feelings never to mention it. When he was home, he and Jimmy went down to the local pub together to have a beer and play darts. Occasionally they went bass fishing off the rocks, a new pastime for Jimmy that he seemed to enjoy.

I did not go with them: I stayed in the

garden with Father and William. Father had aged, and I worried about him, although Jimmy assured me it was only a temporary loss of weight and appetite and that, like me, he would pick up strength as time went by.

Father and I became very close during this time. He talked to me as we sat together on those sunny afternoons, mostly about my mother and their life together. He confessed that these last six months had almost made him thankful she had died before she could see one of the family disgraced. Otherwise, he kept Greg's name out of our conversations and indulged in many recollections of my childhood.

Only Elsie steadfastly refused to welcome Jimmy as a guest at the Folly. Her wrinkled old face scowling, she would indicate his arrival to me by announcing: "That there doctor has called to see 'ee again, Miss Samantha." Her attitude was not unlike Aunt Tibby's — a blind refusal to hear one word against Greg or to believe he would do anything wrong.

Elsie sensed my growing dependence on Jimmy and was once bold enough to say to me: "You be Master Greg's wife, Miss Samantha, and he wouldn't like 'ee spending all your time with that there doctor of 'een."

Once I recovered from what Dr. Edwards called my 'nervous breakdown', Jimmy took me for long drives in his car. One weekend we went to Gloucester where his parents lived to visit his son Peter. The boy was hell-bent on joining the air force, so we took him to an air display. I derived so much pleasure from Peter's excitement that for once I completely forgot myself. The trip was a success, and on the drive home Jimmy dropped his guard sufficiently to tell me how happy he was that Peter and I had taken such a liking to each other.

"I'm aware that you won't want to commit yourself to anything positive yet, Samantha," he said more emotionally than usual, "but you must know I am hoping very much that in time you might consider Peter and myself a part of your life. I'm certain I could make you happy. I *know* you would make us happy. You can't go *on* living in the past forever, my dear."

I was silent, upset by this sudden, renewed expression of his feelings. My nerves screamed in protest. I thought I had successfully stopped myself from feeling emotion of any kind. By not thinking about the past or the future and by never allowing myself to remember Greg locked up in prison, I had even begun to find a certain contentment and peace. Despite my silence Jimmy went on:

"Have you thought any more about divorcing Greg? Your father says it would be easy after all the facts that will come out in court."

Despite the heat, I shivered. Jimmy was touching raw nerves, and I could not stand the pain.

"I don't see that it's any of your business, Jimmy."

I spoke so rudely I would not have blamed him for being furious. But he merely took my hand.

"You *are* my business, Samantha. I love you very much. Everything you do and say and think are important to me."

"But I don't want you to feel like that!" I cried childishly.

"I know. I understand!" Jimmy's voice was quiet and soothing. "But you can't live the rest of your life in a vacuum. Look, darling, you've got to face the future one day soon. You may never quite recover from this disaster. I can understand that, too. But it will, in time, become possible for you to love someone else, even if differently. Just as I've discovered I can love you as much as I ever loved Pamela. Differently, that's all. I am a different person now, older, changed. You

271

are changing, too. Life won't stand still for you, however much you want it to do so."

In my heart I knew he was right. But I was not yet ready for any decision concerning Greg.

I was fond of Jimmy, I depended on him, needed him, respected him. But I was not in love with him.

As if aware of my thoughts, he said:

"I know how you feel about me, Samantha. Half the trouble is that you won't *let* yourself fall in love again. Do you realize that you have not even let me kiss you since the Newquay evenings together?"

His voice was so indignant, I had to smile. Then Jimmy smiled, too, and suddenly we were close once more. I allowed myself to think about kissing him, and surprisingly I wanted it. I wanted to be in someone's arms again, to be held securely, to be desired. I was sick of being alone.

It was dark by the time we reached Tristan's Bay. Jimmy stopped the car at the entrance to the drive and switched off the engine.

"You haven't spoken a word since we stopped for dinner, Samantha, and that was a good hour ago. Are you angry with me for any reason?"

"Oh, no, Jimmy, how could I be? It's been

a lovely day!" I answered truthfully. I felt him relax beside me.

"It's been a wonderful day for me — all of it!" he said softly.

If he had asked me to kiss him, I might have refused. But he took me into his arms as if it were the most natural thing in the world to do. And as naturally, my body responded when his mouth came down on mine. Gently at first; then with passion and hunger his kisses told me how much he loved and wanted me.

I felt my lips open to his. My eyes closed. For a moment or two I was all woman again — a woman who craved for love and a lover. For a brief while I was able to keep the memory of Greg from disturbing me. But as Jimmy's embrace grew more passionate and demanding, I felt suddenly afraid of this love and found myself wondering how to extricate myself from his arms.

Finally I drew away from him breathlessly, pushing my hair back from my forehead.

"I'm afraid I'm a dead loss to you, Jimmy!" I told him with genuine regret. "This really isn't fair to you. I can't give you what you need or deserve."

Jimmy recovered his composure. He touched my cheek with his hand and said:

"No apologies or regrets, remember?

Besides, I knew very well it was just too soon ... that's all. You did want me to kiss you, didn't you, Samantha? So that's a start."

"A start, but with no likelihood of a happy ending!" I said awkwardly, determined to be truthful with him at all costs.

"That's my worry, not yours!"

"It doesn't seem fair to you!" I protested again. "You could be dating other girls who aren't as confused as I am."

"I don't want 'other girls'!" Jimmy said emphatically. "And tell me, Samantha, what exactly are you confused about? I haven't tried to discuss Greg with you because I knew the subject upset you. But if you could tell me what is at the back of your mind, it might clear the air for both of us. On the other hand, if it has nothing to do with Greg, and it's just that you don't really care about me, then ... "

"But I do care about you, Jimmy — a great deal," I broke in. "I'd no idea it was possible to be so fond of someone, so dependent on their friendship and affection and not be in love with them. I suppose it all boils down to the simple fact that I cannot forget Greg. I still love him."

Jimmy lit a cigarette. He smoked very rarely, and I knew that when he did, it was

274

because he was under tension.

"Can you see any solution to the problem of Greg?" he asked gently. "He is certain to be sent to prison for years. By the time he comes out, you'll both be too old to start again. Or are you hoping he might at the eleventh hour decide to put up a defence at his trial? Be found innocent?"

I tried to quell the panic Jimmy's words roused in me. I had not permitted myself to consider such things. Greg wrote to me regularly and as often as regulations allowed, but he never mentioned his trial or discussed revoking his confession of guilt. I felt he had resigned himself to the long years of incarceration ahead of him. His letters were noncommittal. He told me he was adjusting to prison life, that he was thinking about studying Japanese in order to keep his mind active. He said such meaningless things as the food was good, that he got on well with the warders, that the prison governor was an intelligent and likable man. He never once complained about anything, nor did he seem bitter or resentful. He always inquired after my health, told me he appreciated my seeing a lot of poor Aunt Tibby, that he hoped William was more obedient now that I had more time to spend on his training. The only reference to us and to our marriage was at the end of each letter: *'Don't forget me or that I love you and miss you terribly, Greg.'*

But for those last words I might have believed he had given me up as easily as he appeared to have given up his freedom. I might have felt more ready to try to put him out of my life, to start those divorce proceedings that I had so many times considered, then rejected.

Haltingly, I tried to explain all these things to Jimmy. He was frowning when I finally stopped speaking.

"It doesn't seem altogether quite fair of Greg," he said.

This was the first time I had ever heard him criticize Greg, and it shook me. I am sure he felt impelled to voice this criticism for my sake, and would not have done so to further his own ends.

"I feel he is trying to use his love for you to keep you tied to him," Jimmy went on slowly. "And that I cannot understand. If he really does love you, he'd set you free. He's using a sort of emotional blackmail. Does he want you to spend the next decade alone, waiting for him?"

I was silent. There seemed no answer to this, other than that none of Greg's past actions indicated that he had ever considered me, so why should I expect him to do so now. The only exception I could find for him was at the very beginning. Knowing the weakness in his own character, he had postponed our wedding, perhaps meaning to back out of the engagement made on impulse. In retrospect, I could believe that he had tried then just for a little while to put my happiness before his own, knowing himself to be unfit for marriage. He had kept the flaws in his nature so well concealed from me — from all of us — that we had never suspected he was a weak character likely to succumb to any temptation that came his way. Even now, when he had admitted to being a traitor, I could not reconcile this with the Greg I'd known all my life. He had ruined his career and our lives not for a principle, but for easy money. Perhaps the biggest weakness of all was his refusal to defend himself. It was as if he had been saying all along: *'This is the way I am, and if you can't accept me as I am, then there is nothing I can do about it.'* He had never tried to overcome his faults but had simply wandered from one relatively minor lapse into the terrible major one of selling his country's secrets for money.

Least of all could I understand his reaction once he was caught. He had not seemed particularly ashamed. He never once sought to offer excuses for himself. The only time he expressed deep regret was when he said he was sorry he had hurt me, Father, Jolly, Aunt Tibby. It was as though he had no innate sense of honour, no real appreciation of the seriousness of his offences — like a child who sets fire to a house and is sorry you are cross but has no thought for the devastating destruction.

I wondered now, as I sat beside the man I knew in my heart must be worth ten of Greg, how I could love the amoral, immature man I had married. What really made me hesitate to turn my back completely on him and try to begin a new life with Jimmy Planter? The only logical explanation seemed to be that for the whole of my life I had loved Greg, and it had become a habit, as much a part of my daily living as eating or sleeping or breathing. *If I could only break the habit* . . . I thought despairingly.

I turned to Jimmy, told him what I was thinking, tried to make him realize why I was so emotionally crippled.

"I'm not sure if it would work," I said, and my voice faltered. "But perhaps if we could go away together, away from Tristan's Bay, from Cornwall, which is so closely associated with Greg, I might begin to cope with the new concept of caring about someone else. I really want to try to put the past behind me and begin life again. It might be easier for me to make a start in new surroundings. I don't know!"

I felt Jimmy's tenseness as his hand tightened over mine.

"It sounds a most enlightened idea to me!" he said. "I haven't had my summer holiday yet. Let me take you abroad, or to the Highlands. You choose. You would have nothing to fear, you know that. If you wanted the holiday to be platonic, then that's the way it would be."

I felt a lump in my throat. Jimmy's unselfishness always moved me deeply. I said anxiously:

"I couldn't promise anything, Jimmy, except that I would try to let you take our relationship a stage further. I want to force myself to break through this barrier in my mind that won't allow me to be unfaithful to Greg!" I grimaced. "This is beginning to sound like a clinical experiment. I don't mean it that way. I do find you attractive, most attractive. I *want* to feel free to love you, to make love with you. It's just that so far . . ."

"Don't say anymore. I understand perfectly!" Jimmy's voice was reassuring. "You are only repeating what I myself have tried to tell you, that you must give yourself a chance to come to life again. It's enough for me that you are offering me the opportunity to prove that it is possible. And, Samantha darling, don't for one minute feel that you have irrevocably committed yourself to going away with me. If you change your mind at any time between now and when I can get my holiday arranged, you have only to tell me. Understand?"

It was that last generous suggestion that kept me from backing out during the ensuing weeks. There were very many occasions when I found myself nervously regretting the idea. For one thing, I found I was unable to tell Father what I planned to do. I knew that he would disapprove on conventional grounds. I *was* still a married woman, and Father would, I know, gently remind me that I must divorce Greg before I involved myself with Jimmy.

Jolly, on the other hand, was too enthusiastic. His assumption that I was about to close the door on Greg once and for all produced an immediate protest from me. I tried to convince my brother that the planned trip to the Highlands with Jimmy in no way committed me to divorce my husband or to marry Jimmy. But Jolly would have none of that.

"You wouldn't go off with him, Sam, if you hadn't fallen in love!" he said joyfully. "I'm delighted, honestly I am. I like Jim a lot."

I felt terrible.

Then came another letter from Greg with the same unnerving ending: *'Don't forget me or that I love you and miss you terribly.'* I couldn't get the words out of my mind.

Nor could I stop picturing him in prison, locked away from the sunshine, from the world, while I intended to tramp over the sweet-smelling heather on a Scottish moor. He would be ignorant of my intention to betray him. He would imagine me at the Folly, having tea with Father on the terrace, walking William, lunching with Aunt Tibby, shopping in the village. For these were the details I wrote in my letters to him.

A week before I was due to go away with Jimmy I decided that no matter how much it might hurt Greg to know the truth, I must write and tell him exactly what I intended to do and why. For one long sleepless night I wrote and rewrote that letter until finally I reduced the long rambling drafts to basic facts.

Dear Greg

You will remember my telling you that I had become very friendly with one of the doctors at my old hospital. He has been very good to me these past difficult months, and I have grown fond of him. He is in love with me and wants to marry me.

I'm afraid this may upset you and perhaps surprise you as I have not mentioned Jimmy in previous letters for the obvious reason that I did not want to distress you unnecessarily. But I am trying to face a future in which there is little or no possibility of our marriage being anything but a legal formality. I am not in love with Jimmy, but I have decided to go away for two weeks with him so as to find out if I could be happy with him on a permanent basis. If this should prove to be the case, then obviously I will want a divorce.

Since you are not in a position to find out for yourself what I am doing with my life, I feel it is more honest to tell you than to leave you in ignorance. I will, of course, write again after the holiday to tell you what I have decided to do in the long term. It may well be, when you read this, that you yourself will wish to put an end to our marriage. This is for you to decide.

For some time I was unable to make up my mind how to sign my letter. On all the others I had resorted to the uncommitting childish 'With love from Samantha,' but on this occasion the word 'love' seemed more than hypocritical. One did not write what was almost a 'Dear John' letter to one's husband and sign it 'With love.' Yet nothing else seemed appropriate. I could not put 'Best wishes,' nor a far too formal 'Sincerely.' Eventually I resorted once more to simplicity and merely signed my name.

I read the letter through three times before the enormity of it sunk it. It *was* a 'Dear John' letter. How could I possibly ever have considered sending it! It would condemn Greg to what I must assume would be a period of extreme mental distress for no good reason. I had been careful to point out to him that he was in no position to find out my intentions, and I couldn't tell him. Not now. Later, when I knew my own mind. I tore the letter across and dropped it in the wastebasket.

Somehow I forced myself to tell Father a lie, namely, that I was going to Scotland with my friend Peggy. I felt guilty and wretched every time he spoke of the holiday, which he thought an excellent idea. I felt even more miserable when Jolly wrote the day before I left wishing me 'masses of fun' and exhorting me to enjoy myself to the full.

The sight of Jimmy waiting in his car at Newquay bus station reassured me slightly. He looked calm and happy and very handsome in green trousers and a white shirt, his green corduroy jacket draped over the back seat. He jumped out of the car as soon as he saw my bus arrive. He took my suitcase, bent and kissed me lightly as if it were a perfectly natural thing to do. I felt myself relax. I was so tensed up and apprehensive that the slightest wrong move or gesture on Jimmy's part would have sent me careering off home. But he was so natural, so happy, he made me feel the same.

By the time we reached the border, I had few misgivings left. Jimmy succeeded in making me laugh, telling me amusing anecdotes of life in the hospital. Best of all, he made me forget myself and Greg.

The weather was magnificent. We had chosen two weeks when an Indian summer bathed the countryside in sunshine and the air was soft and balmy. A welcome breath of autumn added a breeze to freshen the atmosphere. Jimmy knew the Highlands well and had booked rooms in a small hotel at Kenmore on Loch Tay, a wonderful place to fish for brown trout. The River Tay, which ran from it, was perfect for salmon fishing, and he intended to take me fishing, which he knew I enjoyed.

It was late when we arrived at Kenmore. Despite the hour, we were given a marvellous meal, including fresh salmon. I felt tired but no longer tense as we lingered over our coffee in the lounge, listening to the other guests 'fisherman's' talk as they discussed the day's sport. I did not let myself think of home, of Father, or of the Folly — least of all, of Greg, who would so much have loved this place.

Jimmy decided that I needed an early night and one without any need to make soul-searching decisions. When we went upstairs, he kissed me good night at the door of my room, held me close for a moment, then left me alone.

As I undressed, I thought again what a wonderful person he was and how lucky I was to have someone so kind and considerate to love me. He seemed to know instinctively how I was thinking and feeling.

I went to sleep almost as soon as I got into bed. I slept dreamlessly and woke to see Jimmy, fully dressed, carrying in my breakfast tray.

"Thought you'd like it in bed for a treat!" he said. "It's a real Scottish breakfast — porridge and all!" That set the pattern for the day: friendly, thoughtful, and caring.

That morning we went to see Taymouth Castle, a mile from the village. It was a rather unattractive dull gray stone edifice built by a Scottish duke in Queen Victoria's reign in the hope of persuading the Queen to use it as her official Scottish residence. She preferred Balmoral.

We went for a long walk on the hills, on the north side of Loch Tay. There had been a great deal of reforestry: we found ourselves wandering through fir and pine trees, with the beautiful stretch of water a panoramic sunlit mirror below us.

That evening we had a pleasurable hour in the little hotel bar talking to our fellow guests. The autumn evenings were quite cold, so a big log fire had been lit in the carved stone fireplace. It burned bravely and gave out welcome warmth. Outside in the hall, as I passed through, I was fascinated to see a marble slab on which lay the day's catch — a ten- and an eleven-pound salmon with labels naming the people who had caught them. Jimmy told me these would later be stored in the deep freeze until their owners went home. Meanwhile, the guests who had made the catches were standing drinks all around. I was nervous when Jimmy made the introductions, afraid lest the name Trevellyan spark off any ugly memories. But thoughtful as ever, he introduced me as Miss Jolland, and no eyebrows rose questioningly.

We dined by ourselves, enjoying another very simple but excellent meal. Jimmy chose my favourite wine. Later I had a Cointreau with my coffee. By the time we went upstairs, I was in so mellow and relaxed a frame of mind and body that I accepted it as the most natural thing in the world when Jimmy followed me into my room and sat down on the bed beside me. He took me in his arms and kissed me, at first gently, then with growing passion. I felt my whole body responding.

"It's going to be all right!" I thought, as slowly Jimmy began to undress me. His hands felt firm and cool, and his mouth where it touched my bared shoulders was warm and tender. As his hands moved from my shoulders down to my breasts, his face was very close to mine. I could see my own reflection in his eyes, and it disturbed me, though I did not know why. I must have blinked because Jimmy reached across me and flicked off the light switch. Then he stood up and in the darkness, I heard him undressing. I held my breath, shivering despite the warmth of the room. My nakedness bothered me, and I pulled the bed cover over me. A moment later I felt the weight of Jimmy's body on top of the cover, beside me.

"Samantha?" My name sounded like a question. I wanted to say something, but the words seemed stuck in my throat.

He kissed me, and I put my hands behind his head and kissed him back. But suddenly my body felt numb. I kissed him again and deliberately removed the bed cover that separated us. I could feel the heat of his body as he moved close against me. My own felt rigid. I was aware that he wanted me very much and that he was controlling himself for my sake. I closed my eyes, determined somehow to make myself accept what we both intended to happen. It was desperately important. If I couldn't accept Jimmy as my lover, I couldn't marry him. He knew it, too.

I suppose I could have lain there and pretended. But I felt it would be more cruel to give Jimmy any more hope for the future than I had already done. I didn't have to tell him it had been a mistake, a fiasco. It was no use. Sensitive as always, he held my shivering body, and I felt the hot tears sting my eyes as he began gently to rock me like a child.

"It doesn't matter, darling. It doesn't matter!" he said over and over again.

But it did matter. I hated myself. I hated Greg even more. He had made me his own so completely; ruined me for anyone else, and then deserted me.

"I'm going to divorce Greg. I'm going to forget him and marry you. I love you. I love *you*, Jimmy!" I cried stupidly, frantically.

"Sssh, darling, don't!" he whispered, kissing my wet cheeks and smoothing my damp hair from my forehead. "I won't have you being unhappy about this. It's too soon, that's all. Give it time. I'll wait, even if it takes years. You can't go on loving Greg forever!"

My heart was so full of gratitude mixed with regret and an even stronger feeling, that I did not deserve this man, that I think if he had tried once more to make love to me, I might have responded fully. I don't know, and I never will because he obviously was not prepared to accept me on those terms. He wanted my love, not my body. He told me so. He said the one was only incidental to the other, and until I felt ready to give him both, he would stay satisfied with my friendship and affection.

He left me not long afterward, kissing me good night and tucking the blanket around me as if I were his child. I had never been nearer to loving him, and I told him so. I think when he finally tore himself away, he left in a reasonably happy mood.

I could not sleep. I tossed and turned, wondering what strange quirk of fate could make me stay faithful to a man who had not stayed faithful to me even for a few weeks; what strange twist of the mind could make me long for a man who was a traitor both to his wife and to his country; what misplaced fidelity on my part left me lying here, lonely, frustrated, filled with unsatisfied desire for the man I had married and whom I knew was not worthy to shine the shoes of the one I had just sent away.

Suddenly, there in the darkness, I remembered Father's words:

"You and I are alike, Samantha; when we love, it is for always!"

"No!" I cried, the tears falling fast now. "I don't love him. I don't want him. I don't need him!"

But in my heart was an agonizing, unbearable longing for Greg.

16

Jimmy, as I might have anticipated, made things easy for me the next day. He called at my bedroom to take me down for breakfast. He had already been downstairs to rent fishing rods. The weather was clear, just right for fishing.

I tried to behave naturally, but I found it hard to concentrate. All the time I was thinking that perhaps the fairest thing to Jimmy was for me to cut this holiday short and go home by train.

It wasn't long before Jimmy discovered what was bothering me, and he said instantly:

"I see absolutely no reason whatever for you to leave. That is unless *you* want to go, Samantha. I told you before we came that I was quite prepared to keep our relationship platonic if that is the way you want it, and I haven't changed my mind. So I don't want to hear any more of that 'It isn't fair to you' nonsense. I intend to enjoy my holiday and your company. It's as simple as that."

So on those terms we had a near-perfect fortnight together, fishing, walking, driving, bird watching. I began to feel really fit and much more relaxed. Jimmy never came to my room again but kissed me good night at my door as if this were all he wanted of me.

On our last day, driving home, I could not find words to thank him for making so wonderful a holiday possible. I felt sad and angry with myself for being unable to break with the past. I owed nothing to Greg, and nearly all the happiness I had known since my marriage I owed to Jimmy.

Father was very pleased to have me home. William was ecstatic, and I hugged both of them. Father gave me a long look and said:

"Your holiday has done you good, my dear. You look your old self again."

I'd never been happy about the way I had deceived him. Impulsively I told him there and then that I had not been away with Peggy but with Jimmy Planter. I tried, as best I could, to explain my reasons for going with him and how in the end nothing had happened to change the relationship between Jimmy and myself.

Father never once reproved me. He merely said:

"I'm glad you told me. As for your Jimmy, he sounds an even nicer fellow than I thought. Perhaps the trip was not so ineffectual after all, Sammy. It must have heightened both your affection and your respect for him. It certainly would have done mine."

We left the matter there. I settled down, more or less, to my quiet life at Tristan's Folly. But I was restless and wondered if I ought to try to find work of some kind. I'd no wish to go a long way from home, but I realized I would not find it easy to get suitable employment in the neighbourhood. Eventually I decided I would look for an interesting voluntary job. I didn't need a salary since Father gave me a generous allowance. But I put off making a decision enjoying the last lingering days of fine weather, spending many hours walking William over the cliffs.

Then one morning I became aware I was being followed. I noticed a middle-aged, rather scruffy-looking man always behind me, taking the same paths over the cliffs as I did. I thought nothing of it the first time, but I noticed him again, still carrying binoculars, a day or two later. I wondered if he could be a bird watcher.

On the third occasion that I saw him I was on my way to see Aunt Tibby. I caught sight of him loitering near the sand dunes. I was certain that this was no coincidence. He was definitely following me.

I felt uneasy. Since Greg's trouble there

had been any number of uneducated, unintelligent people who disregarded the fact that his family had had no part in his activities and who wrote us nasty letters, called out objectionable things in the street, threw stones at the house, and generally made our lives unpleasant. Lately this wretched persecution had stopped, but it occurred to me now, seeing the stranger move away behind the dunes as if he did not wish me to know he was following me, that he might well be one of the cranks Father and I had been plagued with in the past.

I was glad of William's company. I hurried toward the Hall, determined to leave Aunt Tibby immediately after tea so that I would get home before dark.

But I did not tell Father about the man, not wishing him to worry before I was really certain he was shadowing me: Next day I saw him again, leaning against a stone wall pretending to read a newspaper as I walked past him on my way to the village. And that evening William barked and pulled heavily on his leash as I took him down the drive for a last outing before bedtime. I had no doubt there was someone lurking in the shrubbery, but I was too frightened to look. I almost let William chase the prowler but decided this might push the man into acting out whatever crazy notion he had to upset or injure me.

I turned back and forced myself to walk up to the house at my usual pace. But my heart was thumping, and as soon as I shut the front door behind me, I ran to the library to tell Father. He listened quietly, then went straight to the telephone to ring the police. He came back, his face flushed and angry.

"That new fellow who has replaced our old inspector had the damned cheek to suggest we can't complain if we are followed about or plagued. I gave him the rough edge of my tongue, and he changed his tune and said he'd send Penrith to have a word with us. He's quite a good lad. The inspector says you're to give him a full description of the fellow who's following you; then they'll check up."

I felt relieved. Probably the prowler would disappear before Penrith reached us, but at least I felt a little less unnerved now that we had the law keeping an eye on us.

Father went off to make sure that all the doors and windows were securely locked. Later, Penrith, a nice rosy-cheeked Cornish lad, came up on his bicycle. I told him all I could. He was very civil and sympathetic and went out to have a look around but said he could find no traces of the man.

"I'll keep an eye on the Folly, zur," he

told Father. "Pity you're so far off the beaten track. We're a bit shorthanded at the station, but if you see anything suspicious, or if Miss — I mean Missus" (he deliberately left out Greg's surname) "do get followed again, let us know at once."

But the man stayed away for the next two or three days. I began to wonder if my somewhat vivid imagination had been playing tricks with me and that the man I had seen had not intended to dog my footsteps nor intended me any harm. Then late one afternoon on my way back from Trevellyan Hall I saw him again.

Perhaps because it was almost at the same point where I had met the unpleasant-looking Mr. Richards that I was reminded of him. Although this man bore no resemblance to Greg's one-time friend, I found myself wondering if this were another of Greg's peculiar associates.

I reached the Folly without harm but thoroughly uneasy. I tried to hide my growing nervousness from Father. For several days I continued to catch glimpses of the man in the distance. He was always looking in my direction, as if he had been given instructions not to let me out of his sight. I became more and more jumpy. Jimmy remarked on it when he came to spend Sunday with us.

"Nothing wrong, Samantha, is there?" he asked when we went for a walk that afternoon. "You seem terribly on edge!"

"No, nothing at all," I lied.

I did not want to sound ridiculous, and I had begun to feel more than a little uneasy because no one but me had ever noticed the strange man. The summer visitors had long since departed, and it was rare to see a stranger in or around Tristan's Bay. The odd one who did come was usually noticed and discussed, and Elsie always heard the village gossip. I had mentioned the man with the binoculars to her, but she knew nothing of him. Could he be some strange figment of my imagination? Could I be going a little crazy? I knew that prolonged and intense nervous strain could affect the mind quite severely. I had been through a lot this past year, since Greg had asked me to marry him. Except for that brief respite in Scotland with Jimmy, I had not been mentally at peace for a long time.

Once the idea that I might not be quite sane was in my head, I began remembering silly little incidents that had seemed unimportant at the time: the coffee I had purchased and left behind in the village shop; the teapot and saucer I had broken when I was helping Elsie; the letter I had posted for Aunt Tibby without remembering to put a stamp on it.

With Jimmy holding my hand as we walked over the headland, I had nothing to fear from the real (or imaginary) man, so I took the opportunity to watch for him. I thought, if he appeared, I would walk toward him and, if I could get near enough, ask him what he was doing wandering around Tristan's Bay, why he was following me. But he gave me no such opportunity to confront him, staying invisible.

When Jimmy returned to the hospital, I felt even more depressed, more uncertain whether the man was real. Father noticed how restless I was that evening. He suggested during dinner that I might like to move from my solitary turret room to the dressing room adjoining his bedroom.

"If anything strange should happen in the night," he said, "there would be no one near enough to the turret to hear you call out. I should have thought of it sooner. You can't like being all alone up there."

"That's ridiculous!" I said, my tone sharp and irritable. It frightened me that Father had noticed something unusual in my manner. "I've slept alone up there for most of my life and not been afraid."

"Just as you like, my dear!" he said soothingly, but he looked at me with concern, and this added to my now serious belief that I was not behaving like a normal person. I wished I had told Jimmy how I felt. He could at least have given me a doctor's opinion as to my state of mind. I resolved to have a frank talk with him next time I saw him. Maybe he'd suggest I go to a psychiatrist. I was beginning to believe I needed one!

That night I found it impossible to get to sleep. I tossed restlessly for hours until my bed was so disturbed I could find no smooth place to lie on. I thought a storm might be brewing. Far below I could hear the waves pounding on the rocks. I burrowed deeper beneath the bedclothes. I was often lonely, but tonight I felt unbearably so. I tried to shut out the memory of Greg, but to no avail. I would have given the whole of the rest of my life just to be lying in his arms again. Greg had failed me utterly as a husband, but he had never failed me as my lover. Apart from the carefree happiness of our childhood, our loving was all we ever had shared. I refused to believe even now that he had belonged to Jane Swan as he had to me, heart and soul.

The thought of Greg's mistress did at least have the effect of subduing my longing for him. My thoughts turned once more to the man who had been following me. I feared that he was evil and had come to destroy my mind. Or else to kill me. As at last I fell asleep, his image was very much on my mind. I knew quite certainly that he was not very far away.

17

I woke in the middle of the night without knowing why. A strong wind was howling against the walls, but there was no rain. Through the parted curtains I could see a bright full moon. White clouds were scurrying over its face and billowing across the sky.

Downstairs, William barked; once, twice. Then I heard a stone rattle against my windowpane. Still half asleep I thought at first that it might be a lone sea gull blown by the wind against the building. But when a second stone hit the glass with a sharp crack, I knew it was no gull. I heard William bark again and then give a faint, prolonged howl. I was suddenly afraid. Someone was outside on the terrace throwing stones at my window.

I lay stiff and silent beneath the bedclothes, wondering if I were imagining this, too. A third stone hit the window. I was reminded of my childhood and the time Greg and Jolly decided to have a midnight picnic on the beach. They had intended to go without me but at the last minute weakened and flung pebbles at my window to call me down to join them.

Greg! I thought. But it could not be him, not unless . . .

I jumped out of bed and ran across to the window. Down below I could see two dark figures muffled in heavy duffel coats. One of them looked so like Greg that my heart began to hammer furiously. But it *could* not be. Greg was locked up in prison.

An arm lifted and beckoned me to go down, then pointed to the kitchen door. Whoever the prowlers were, they knew the layout and wished to be let into the house. But *who* would arrive like this in the middle of the night. If they were legitimate visitors, why not ring the front doorbell? Whoever they were, they came stealthily. And that could *only* mean Greg, Greg on the run?

I pulled on my dressing gown and slippers. My heart pounded. I intended to hurry down and open the door, but I hesitated and slowed down as I reached the hall.

If it were Greg, I told myself, I would not help him escape. He would almost certainly be caught again, and it would not help his cause. If it *were* Greg, I had to talk to him, convince him he must give himself up.

My heart doubled its beat. I shivered violently. It seemed so very, very long since I had seen Greg, and no matter how terrible his crime might prove to be, he was still my husband. I still loved him. I longed to be held just once more in his arms. I reached the kitchen. William bounded out of his basket and ran from me to the back door, whining continuously. I quieted him as best I could, afraid he would wake Elsie, whose room was at the end of the passage. The kitchen was warm, but I was ice cold as I stood hesitantly with my hand on the heavy iron bolt. I was remembering Father's words:

"He's no good, Sam, and you've just got to face up to it. Greg is the rotten apple in the Trevellyan barrel. You'll have to get rid of him, my dear."

I remembered Jolly's advice:

"You can't possibly love him *now*, Sam. He'll be found guilty, and it'll be years and years before they set him free. And when they do, probably he will defect to the other side. You wouldn't want to go with him, would you? So there's no point in you waiting for him."

I remembered my reply:

"I'm not sure, Jolly. If Greg were free . . . "

"Then you should be sure," Jolly had interrupted me. "Even if you don't care about the disgrace for yourself, you wouldn't want to give your children a traitor for a father."

I remembered also Jimmy's urgent plea:

"Darling, you know now that you misjudged Greg's character. Don't you see that you may as easily have misjudged *your* feelings for him? You were conditioned in your childhood into believing you loved him. But you never really had a chance to see him objectively. Come away with me; give me a chance to show you that you can fall in love again."

It had all sounded so simple. All I had to do was to stop caring about Greg. Yet if it *were* Greg out there in the darkness, needing me . . . My hand tightened on the bolt. I drew it back swiftly.

The door swung open, and Greg pushed past me, his companion close behind him. Strangely, I was not surprised to recognize Mr. Richards. I assumed without question that he was a confederate of Greg's, perhaps the very person who had first led Greg astray and no doubt had helped him to escape from detention now.

For a desperate moment Greg and I looked at each other.

"Quick, into the library!" Greg said, turning out the light so that we were plunged in darkness. "Elsie mustn't know we are here. It's *vital*, Sam. Understand?"

I understood very well. Greg wanted my

help and expected me to join him in this getaway. He took my compliance for granted, I followed Greg and Richards up the hall into the library. I wondered what Greg would do if Father suddenly came in. Then Greg switched on the reading lamp by Father's leather chair, and I really saw him properly for the first time.

"Oh, Greg!" I whispered. The words caught in my throat as I saw how painfully thin and haggard he looked. His face was the very epitome of suffering. Yet incredibly he was smiling.

"Sam!" he said. "Oh, Sam!"

The next minute I was in his arms. I didn't care about Richards. I didn't care if Father came in. I didn't care about anything but Greg. I loved him. It did not seem possible I could ever have doubted it. I loved him no matter what he had done; no matter what he was. And he loved me.

"Darling, darling, *darling!*"

His words were caresses, and his kisses fell on my lips, my hair, my cheeks. Mr. Richards, surprisingly tactful, was keeping the excited William away from us, his back turned as he tried to calm the dog.

Then the library door opened, and Father came in.

I stiffened instinctively, but Greg kept his

arms about me, even when Father spoke to Greg in a harsh voice I had never in my life heard before.

"Get out of my house, Greg Trevellyan, or I shall call the police!"

I felt hot, then cold. My teeth started to chatter.

"Father, *please!*" I began, but Greg silenced me: he placed his hand gently over my mouth.

"It's all right, Sam. Let me do the explaining. Sir, this gentleman is from Intelligence. He very kindly drove me down here. He can show you his credentials and will confirm what I have to tell you. I was afraid you wouldn't believe me if I came alone. My story is so fantastic."

I stared at him, wondering why I had not heard a car in the drive, though my room was at the front of the house. Greg's next words explained this.

"We left our car hidden by the sand dunes and walked up here," he said. "It is really very, *very* important that no one but you, sir, and Sam should know we are here. Could we all sit down while I explain?"

Father hesitated. Something in Greg's voice, calm and authoritative, must have convinced him that Greg was not just making a break for freedom. Assuredly he did not look nervous or hunted. On the contrary, he seemed amazingly cool and sure of himself. After a pause Father nodded. Greg drew me onto the sofa, holding my hand tightly. Mr. Richards seated himself in the chair opposite Father.

At the start of Greg's story, I did find myself wondering if I could possibly be dreaming. But as the words came pouring out, I knew that every word was true. My heart began to sing.

"It was the week before Sam and I had arranged our wedding in Trevellyan church," Greg said, "when Richards first approached me. He told me he wanted me to do something for my country which Intelligence felt to be vital."

Mr. Richards smiled faintly. I still could not reconcile myself to the idea that this man was not an enemy, although when he smiled he looked a little less like a weasel.

"That's an understatement, if I may interrupt," he broke in on Greg. "You see, Commander, Mrs. Trevellyan, we happened to know that the Russians were very anxious to get some up-to-date data on the newest American submarine. Trevellyan, your son Jolland, and their fellow officers were, as you probably know, training for eventual operation of these subs. We knew the

Russians had a man in Trenoun whose job was to supply any information he could acquire. I was detailed to keep an eye on him, and general security. That's when I singled out your husband, Madam — " he smiled faintly at me — "as someone who could be of great help to us."

"I don't understand," I said. "How could Greg help?"

"By playing the part of a traitor. But first he had to discredit himself sufficiently to convince their agent that he was a likely person to sell them information."

My father spoke for the first time.

"And the information Greg was to sell to the enemy — it would be false?"

"In part," Mr. Richards nodded. "Facts we knew the Russians already had would be real, but other vital information would be fractionally wrong — enough to mislead them when working out any invention to upset the new submarine's performance."

Greg turned now to look at me.

"You can imagine, darling, what a terrible predicament this put me in. You and I were already engaged, planning our wedding. If I agreed to help the way Richards wanted, I knew I'd have to discredit myself not just in the world's eyes but in yours, too. When Intelligence picked me for the job, they didn't know about you — about us."

I was beginning to understand at last.

"So *that's* why you called off the wedding!"

Greg nodded. "I felt it was too unfair to you to go ahead with it." He sighed. "But I wasn't able to go on being so noble. I loved you too much, Sam. I was afraid if we didn't get married, you'd go off and find someone else, and it could have been years before I was free to tell you the truth. I know now it was selfish and cruel, but I *had* to be sure you were mine and then just trust to providence that when the storm broke, your love for me would be great enough to go on believing in me."

I felt suddenly distraught.

"Oh, Greg. And I failed!" I cried, covering my face with my hands.

Gently Greg pulled my hands away and stroked my cheek.

"Darling, you did no such thing. You didn't walk out on me because of Jane Swan. Some wives would have divorced their husbands for less. Of course, Jane was in on the act. My so-called affair with her was the chosen way of discrediting me."

"So you never . . . "

"No, I never!" Greg interrupted, smiling. "One day you must meet Jane, darling. She's a very courageous and patriotic woman. You'll like her."

I swallowed several times. My throat felt dry, and my face burned.

"I'm so ashamed!" I whispered.

Father coughed. I could see the relief on his face.

"If this is so, I owe you an apology, Greg," he said. "I'm afraid I did my best to encourage Samantha to finish with you."

"You're not to blame, sir. Nor is she. Nor Jolly. As far as *he* was concerned, I really wanted him to break with me so that there'd be no stain against his name when I was finally disgraced. Fortunately, that worked out very well. It would not have made me in the least bit happy if Jolly had insisted on remaining my friend to the bitter end. But as far as Sam goes, darling, when I got your letter telling me you intended going away with your doctor . . . "

"But Greg," I interrupted. "I never sent that letter. I thought . . . "

"I guessed as much!" Greg interrupted me now. "But you forgot my faithful friend, Elsie. The old dear was afraid you'd end up marrying your doctor. When she found that letter in the wastebasket, (and read it, the old rascal), she thought it was high time I knew what was going on. It didn't seem to cross her mind I was locked up in prison because she sent it to me and wrote, "Do 'ee cum right on home, Master Greg, and see after Miss Samantha."

He imitated her voice so well I had to smile, although I was shocked to think of Greg's feelings when he received my letter.

"Thank goodness she did send it!" Greg went on. "Frankly, I was already regretting my patriotic self-sacrifice. I must have been mad ever to consider it, although I was promised I wouldn't stay locked up indefinitely! Your letter galvanized me into action. I just had to be free. I couldn't act the hero any longer." Mr. Richards raised his brows and nodded, his tight lips smiling slightly.

"Trevellyan got in touch with us and told us we'd better do something quickly or he'd spill the beans, Russians or no Russians! Fortunately for your husband, we had just learned from our counterparts in America that the Russians have caught up with them and are now sufficiently far advanced with the new scientific techniques to produce similarly powered vessels of their own." He smiled at me kindly. "So it's only a matter of time before the submarine at H.M.S. Trenoun will be off the secret list and Greg's activities of little interest to anyone anymore."

"You mean — Greg's free?" I asked incredulously.

"Well, not exactly," Mr. Richards answered. "We appreciate we owe it to this young man to do something to help, so we decided the time had come to 'spring' him. In ordinary parlance, we fixed an escape. Greg is now 'on the run' and will be assumed for the time being to have defected. In actual fact, he'll shortly be starting a new life in Australia."

My heart felt like a stone. Greg would be going to a country thousands of miles away. We were to be separated again. It was unbearable.

Seeing my face, Greg laughed.

"Don't look so miserable, darling. *You're coming with me!* That is, if you want to. That's why Richards and I have come here tonight, despite the risk of my being seen and re-arrested. I couldn't be sure, you see, whether or not you'd fallen in love with this man, Jimmy Planter."

I suppose it was stupid, but I burst into tears. Father decided tactfully that it was time to offer Mr. Richards a drink and took him off to the dining room. Greg drew me into his arms and let me cry for a few minutes. Then he gave me his old grin, which I hadn't seen for so long, and said:

"I hope you are crying for poor Jimmy and not for poor me!"

I hugged him despairingly.

"Oh, Greg! I've been such a fool. I've always loved you. I tried not to. I wanted to love Jimmy. He's been marvellous to me. It would all have been so simple if I could only have stopped wanting *you*, Greg!" I looked at him, horrified by the memory of how nearly I had betrayed him. "Greg, I did go away with Jimmy. I *meant* to be unfaithful. I really tried, and then at the last minute — it was awful. I felt so mean."

"Yes, I understand!" Greg said. "But don't blame yourself, Sam. Your instincts were right. The evidence was hopelessly weighted against me. I'm sure your doctor is a nice chap, and you kept faith in your heart if not in your mind."

"Aunt Tibby has kept faith all the way along!" I whispered, ashamed.

Greg grinned again.

"Don't you believe it. She may not have let on to you, but I've never stopped receiving the sharp edge of her tongue both before and while I've been in prison. You should have read her letters! She was just too proud to admit to anyone, even you, that I'd failed

313

her. Poor Aunt Tib!"

I looked at him aghast.

"But what will happen to her now? She'll believe you really have defected!"

"Don't worry about that. I have permission for your father and Aunt Tibby to be told the facts. They were pretty reluctant at first, but I told them that you would never leave your father without telling him where you were going and that it might kill my poor aunt. So they relented, although your father isn't allowed to give her the information until after we're in Australia. Even then, she isn't to know *where* we are. Not that she'll care once she knows I'm not the scoundrel I was supposed to be."

I took a deep breath. This was all too much to take in.

"What about your future?" I asked. "Your career in the navy, Greg? As you've been working for England, it isn't fair that you should have to hide yourself away for the rest of your life."

"It won't be for that long!" Greg said, and drew away from me for a moment to light a cigarette. "Just as soon as the sub comes off the secret list, we can come home. Perhaps a year, two at the most. Then I'll probably be showered with belated honours and, I hope, fully vindicated. Your father, and Aunt Tibby, and the village, and poor old Jolly will all be able to hold up their heads again."

I let this sink in. Then I said:

"What will we do in Australia, Greg? Where will we live?"

"I'm being given enough money to buy a business. If you approve of the idea, we'll go to the coast and run a sailing club. We can live in a sumptuous house near the sea — under assumed names, of course." He laid his hand against my cheek and looked at me with a strange shyness. "I thought — that is, once I was sure you'd be coming with me, I thought we might possibly start a family."

The tears began to fall again. I quickly told Greg that I wasn't unhappy, just overcome. I understood now why he had been so appalled when I had told him I was going to have a baby. It was good to know that in ordinary circumstances, he would have been as thrilled as I was.

"If only you could have told me the truth right from the start!" I whispered.

"I know! But it would have been too dangerous, Sam. In a way, you've played a large part in what I've tried to do for poor old England. It was so essential you should look miserable and behave as you did, finally showing your contempt. If anyone deserves a medal, you do, darling. I think you probably suffered more than I did. Was I wrong, Sam, to put you through such a terrible ordeal? If you had been asked before, would you have told me to agree to play the part? Should I not have married you?"

"I don't know!" I said truthfully. "But I'm glad you did, though right now the only thing I can think of is that I pray to God it never happens again!"

"It won't. It can't," Greg said simply. "Moreover, I'll be a family man by the time this has all blown over. I would never have agreed to this assignment if I'd already been a father. Somehow I had enough faith in you to feel sure you wouldn't forsake me. If I hadn't felt that way, I don't think I would have agreed to do what I did."

"I nearly, so nearly did forsake you!" I whispered. The thought was unbearable.

"Nearly isn't nearly enough, as old Elsie is always saying!"

I thought suddenly of the man who had been following me. Greg smiled when I asked him if my shadow had been a Russian agent.

"Definitely not! The Russians lost all interest in H.M.S. Trenoun and me as soon as they had the information they thought they needed. No, darling, your mysterious prowler was one of Richards' men keeping an eye on your movements. They wanted to be sure you were at home when the right moment came for me to make my 'escape' to collect you. Imagine if I'd called here tonight and you'd been in Scotland!"

"Greg, don't!" I begged him.

He took me in his arms, but before he kissed me, I held him away from me so that I could really look at him. It was so wonderful to see him once again as the laughing young man I had worshipped all my youth. And he had proved himself a real hero. Now that I knew the truth at last, I was shattered by the knowledge that I had doubted him.

"Forgive me. *Forgive me!*" I begged.

"If you still love me, there is nothing, *nothing* to forgive!" Greg said, and this time I did not try to stop him kissing me.

When Father returned to the library, I noticed that he, too, looked his old self. His face was beaming, and when he shook hands with Greg, he apologized again for doubting him.

"You were always like a second son to me, Greg, and I was so deeply hurt when . . ."

"Don't think any more about it," Greg said quickly. "After all, I did confess to everything I was accused of. You had every reason to condemn me, and now you're going to have to forgive me. I'm taking Sam away from you. We may be gone some time."

"I know!" Father said gruffly. "Richards has explained all the details to me. I'll go and see Tibby just as soon as it is permitted. And don't worry about her, my boy, I'll soon put an end to her stupid veto against me. By the time you come back, Tib and I will be the best of friends. That's a promise."

I flung myself into Father's arms, and he gave me a quick hug.

"Off you go and pack," he said. "You've got to be away in half an hour."

"In half an hour!" I gasped.

It was Mr. Richards' turn to do some explaining.

"It may sound a little complicated for you to digest all at once," he said, looking at me kindly. "So I'll make it as simple as I can. The most important aspect of all this planning is that the Russians should go on believing for some time yet that Greg is an unpatriotic weakling who sold out his country's secrets for money. He was too small fry for them to have bothered about him when he was caught, but they might think it strange that having 'escaped,' he does not turn to them for help in getting out of the country. It would be the obvious thing for him to do if he'd really been helping them. Do you understand me so far?"

I nodded.

"So we have had to devise a very good reason for Greg to go to Australia. Two weeks ago we put one of our chaps in jail on a fake forgery charge, in cooperation with the police, of course. The background we gave him was of a rich Australian crook. We arranged for him to be put in a cell near Greg's and for them to rapidly become friendly. The two were heard by their fellow prisoners to be planning an escape so that when eventually they succeeded in getting away, news of their conspiracy would leak out to the underworld and, so we hope, to any Russians still interested enough to check on Greg's activities. They are very thorough as a rule."

"An ingenious plan!" Father said approvingly.

"The supposed crook is providing the money to pay for a yacht," Mr. Richards went on. "Greg is to go with him because of his particular knowledge of sailing."

Greg grinned down at me.

"Let's hope I haven't forgotten my yachting techniques!" he said. "Because that's not fiction, Sam. In an hour or two we'll be halfway across the Channel. The yacht is waiting for us in a small bay near Falmouth. Richards will be driving us there as soon as you are packed."

I tried to keep calm, but I was becoming more excited every minute. Stupidly, I said:

"But I don't know what to pack!"

"What about that trousseau of yours?" Father suggested, smiling. "Time you wore some of those clothes instead of weeping over them. Greg always said he'd take you on a honeymoon one day. What better occasion than this!"

I tore upstairs in a sudden whirl of activity. I felt on fire with excitement. My clothes lay neatly folded between layers of tissue paper in Father's sea chest. It was a simple matter to transfer them to my suitcase. Hurriedly I made up my face, combed my hair, and put on black slacks and a white pullover. When I saw my reflection in the mirror, I was quite startled by my own transformation. It was the face of a glowing woman with deep joy in her eyes instead of that other sad, embittered girl who thought she had lost her husband and lover for ever. A magical new life stretched in front of me. I looked around the disordered room and paused, realizing that it might be a very long time before I entered it again.

Then I smiled. This was the home of my childhood. I was in truth grown up now,

Greg's wife at last. From now on my home would be with him.

I stopped only long enough to pack the framed photo of Father, my mother, and Jolly that stood on my mantelpiece. I nearly added the photo of Greg, tall, fair, smiling, as a young man leaning up against the side of a fishing boat, wearing jeans and a polo-necked sweater. I had always loved it, for it so perfectly epitomized Greg. But I laid it down again. I wouldn't need that to remind me of the boy Greg had once been, nor of the man he had become. I was going with him to begin a new life. Father and Aunt Tibby and William would console each other.

Suddenly, I remembered Jimmy, and my heart sank. I had no way by which I could warn him that I was about to go out of his life for years, if not forever; no way to thank him for being such a good friend, for saying how sorry I was that his story could not end as perfectly as my own.

My diary lay on my desk, unfinished. Seeing it, I knew that I would never again want it and that perhaps Jimmy would like to read it, to see in my own writing how much I had needed him, depended on him, how very, very fond of him I was.

Hurriedly, I reached for my pen and added a few last lines.

Please don't be sad that I'm going away with Greg. I think I just had to go on loving him no matter what he did. And no matter how hard I tried, I would never have been a good wife to you because I could never have given you the love you need and so much deserve. I hope it won't be long before you and Peter find someone to look after you. I will never forget you. Thank you, Jimmy, and bless you, dear,

Samantha

I put it in an envelope. When I went downstairs I would give it to Father to hand over to Jimmy when Mr. Richards said it would be in order to do so. Though Jimmy would not know where I was or why, he would at least know that I hadn't gone out of his life without giving him an assurance of my deep gratitude and friendship.

I looked up to see Greg standing in the doorway watching me.

"Sad?" he asked.

I shook my head and ran into his arms.

"I'm the happiest girl in the whole world!" I said, and pressed my cheek against his.

Greg held my hand tightly when we drove away from Tristan's Folly. Through a mist of tears I could see the house and what I thought might be Father's lonely figure on the terrace outlined against the brilliant moonlit sky. As we passed the Hall, Greg said softly:

"It's good to think your father and Aunt Tib will comfort each other and be friends again. You and I, Sam, will have brought them together. I don't like to think of your father all alone without you."

I nodded, but I was aware of what Greg did not realize, that Father would always be alone because my mother, his only love, was dead. No one could replace her, just as no one could replace Greg; whom I'd believed was lost to me forever.

"We'll be together always!" Greg whispered, as if he had read my thoughts.

I nodded, leaning closer to him, knowing that I, like Tristan's Folly, had withstood the onslaught of the storm.

THE END

THE GREENWAY
Jane Adams

When Cassie and her twelve-year-old cousin Suzie had taken a short cut through an ancient Norfolk pathway, Suzie had simply vanished . . . Twenty years on, Cassie is still tormented by nightmares. She returns to Norfolk, determined to solve the mystery.

FORTY YEARS
ON THE WILD FRONTIER
Carl Breihan & W. Montgomery

Noted Western historian Carl Breihan has culled from the handwritten diaries of John Montgomery, grandfather of co-author Wayne Montgomery, new facts about Wyatt Earp, Doc Holliday, Bat Masterson and other famous and infamous men and women who gained notoriety when the Western Frontier was opened up.

TAKE NOW, PAY LATER
Joanna Dessau

This fiction based on fact is the love-turning-to-hate story of Robert Carr, Earl of Somerset, and his wife, Frances.

McLEAN AT THE GOLDEN OWL
George Goodchild
Inspector McLean has resigned from Scotland Yard's CID and has opened an office in Wimpole Street. With the help of his able assistant, Tiny, he solves many crimes, including those of kidnapping, murder and poisoning.

KATE WEATHERBY
Anne Goring
Derbyshire, 1849: The Hunter family are the arrogant, powerful masters of Clough Grange. Their feuds are sparked by a generation of guilt, despair and ill-fortune. But their passions are awakened by the arrival of nineteen-year-old Kate Weatherby.

A VENETIAN RECKONING
Donna Leon
When the body of a prominent international lawyer is found in the carriage of an intercity train, Commissario Guido Brunetti begins to dig deeper into the secret lives of the once great and good.

A TASTE FOR DEATH
Peter O'Donnell

Modesty Blaise and Willie Garvin take on impossible odds in the shape of Simon Delicata, the man with a taste for death, and Swordmaster, Wenczel, in a terrifying duel. Finally, in the Sahara desert, the intrepid pair must summon every killing skill to survive.

SEVEN DAYS FROM MIDNIGHT
Rona Randall

In the Comet Theatre, London, seven people have good reason for wanting beautiful Maxine Culver out of the way. Each one has reason to fear her blackmail. But whose shadow is it that lurks in the wings, waiting to silence her once and for all?

QUEEN OF THE ELEPHANTS
Mark Shand

Mark Shand knows about the ways of elephants, but he is no match for the tiny Parbati Barua, the daughter of India's greatest expert on the Asian elephant, the late Prince of Gauripur, who taught her everything. Shand sought out Parbati to take part in a film about the plight of the wild herds today in north-east India.

THE DARKENING LEAF
Caroline Stickland

On storm-tossed Chesil Bank in 1847, the young lovers, Philobeth and Frederick, prevent wreckers mutilating the apparent corpse of a young woman. Discovering she is still alive, Frederick takes her to his grandmother's home. But the rescue is to have violent and far-reaching effects . . .

A WOMAN'S TOUCH
Emma Stirling

When Fenn went to stay on her uncle's farm in Africa, the lovely Helena Starr seemed to resent her — especially when Dr Jason Kemp agreed to Fenn helping in his bush hospital. Though it seemed Jason saw Fenn as little more than a child, her feelings for him were those of a woman.

A DEAD GIVEAWAY
Various Authors

This book offers the perfect opportunity to sample the skills of five of the finest writers of crime fiction — Clare Curzon, Gillian Linscott, Peter Lovesey, Dorothy Simpson and Margaret Yorke.

DOUBLE INDEMNITY — MURDER FOR INSURANCE
Jad Adams

This is a collection of true cases of murderers who insured their victims then killed them — or attempted to. Each tense, compelling account tells a story of cold-blooded plotting and elaborate deception.

THE PEARLS OF COROMANDEL
By Keron Bhattacharya

John Sugden, an ambitious young Oxford graduate, joins the Indian Civil Service in the early 1920s and goes to uphold the British Raj. But he falls in love with a young Hindu girl and finds his loyalties tragically divided.

WHITE HARVEST
Louis Charbonneau

Kathy McNeely, a marine biologist, sets out for Alaska to carry out important research. But when she stumbles upon an illegal ivory poaching operation that is threatening the world's walrus population, she soon realises that she will have to survive more than the harsh elements . . .

TO THE GARDEN ALONE
Eve Ebbett
Widow Frances Morley's short, happy marriage was childless, and in a succession of borders she attempts to build a substitute relationship for the husband and family she does not have. Over all hovers the shadow of the man who terrorized her childhood.

CONTRASTS
Rowan Edwards
Julia had her life beautifully planned — she was building a thriving pottery business as well as sharing her home with her friend Pippa, and having fun owning a goat. But the goat's problems brought the new local vet, Sebastian Trent, into their lives.

MY OLD MAN AND THE SEA
David and Daniel Hays
Some fathers and sons go fishing together. David and Daniel Hays decided to sail a tiny boat seventeen thousand miles to the bottom of the world and back. Together, they weave a story of travel, adventure, and difficult, sometimes terrifying, sailing.

SQUEAKY CLEAN
James Pattinson

An important attribute of a prospective candidate for the United States presidency is not to have any dirt in your background which an eager muckraker can dig up. Senator William S. Gallicauder appeared to fit the bill perfectly. But then a skeleton came rattling out of an English cupboard.

NIGHT MOVES
Alan Scholefield

It was the first case that Macrae and Silver had worked on together. Malcolm Underdown had brutally stabbed to death Edward Craig and had attempted to murder Craig's fiancée, Jane Harrison. He swore he would be back for her. Now, four years later, he has simply walked from the mental hospital. Macrae and Silver must get to him — before he gets to Jane.

GREATEST CAT STORIES
Various Authors

Each story in this collection is chosen to show the cat at its best. James Herriot relates a tale about two of his cats. Stella Whitelaw has written a very funny story about a lion. Other stories provide examples of courageous, clever and lucky cats.